PRAISE FOR

CIRCLE IN THE WATER
AND MARCIA MULLER

*Recipient of the Private Eye Writers of
America Lifetime Achievement Award
And the Mystery Writers of
America Grand Master Award*

"Once again, Muller combines a heartfelt…investigation
with strong elements of a family reunion."
—*Kirkus Reviews*

"Fans of Muller's San Francisco–based PI Sharon McCone
(last seen in *Ice and Stone*, 2021) will be delighted that
the hardworking sleuth is back in another action-packed
adventure…McCone cracks the twist-filled case with her
usual skill and persistence, offering a satisfying conclusion
to a challenging assignment." —*Booklist*

"Muller's McCone set the standard for fictional women
detectives." —*Library Journal*

"One of the world's premier mystery writers."
—*Cleveland Plain Dealer*

CIRCLE
IN THE
WATER

CIRCLE
IN THE
WATER

Marcia Muller

GRAND
CENTRAL

NEW YORK   BOSTON

Copyright © 2024 by Pronzini-Muller Family Trust
Excerpt from *Ice and Stone* copyright © 2021 by Pronzini-Muller Family Trust

Cover design by Jezneel Ross
Cover photo by Marion Mou
Cover copyright © 2024 by Hachette Book Group, Inc.

Grand Central Publishing
Hachette Book Group
1290 Avenue of the Americas, New York, NY 10104
grandcentralpublishing.com
@grandcentralpub

Originally published in hardcover and ebook by Grand Central Publishing in April 2024
First Trade Paperback Edition: November 2024

Grand Central Publishing is a division of Hachette Book Group, Inc. The Grand Central Publishing name and logo is a trademark of Hachette Book Group, Inc.

The publisher is not responsible for websites (or their content) that are not owned by the publisher.

Grand Central Publishing books may be purchased in bulk for business, educational, or promotional use. For information, please contact your local bookseller or the Hachette Book Group Special Markets Department at special.markets@hbgusa.com.

Library of Congress Cataloging-in-Publication Data

Names: Muller, Marcia, author.
Title: Circle in the water / Marcia Muller.
Description: First edition. | New York : Grand Central Publishing, 2024. |
  Series: Sharon McCone mysteries
Identifiers: LCCN 2023041043 | ISBN 9781538724521 (hardcover) | ISBN
  9781538724545 (e-book)
Subjects: LCGFT: Detective and mystery fiction. | Novels.
Classification: LCC PS3563.U397 C57 2024 | DDC 813/.54—dc23/
  eng/20230927
LC record available at https://lccn.loc.gov/2023041043

ISBN: 9781538724521 (hardcover), 9781538724545 (ebook),
      9781538724538 (trade paperback)

Printed in the United States of America

LSC

Printing 1, 2024

*For my readers, who have abetted Sharon
McCone in her long career,
and for Bill, with love*

With special thanks to Melissa Ward

Glory is like a circle in the water,
Which never ceaseth to enlarge itself
Till by broad spreading it disperse to naught.
— William Shakespeare, *Henry VI, Part 1*

CIRCLE
IN THE
WATER

While most of its streets are owned by the city, San Francisco boasts more than two hundred that are in the hands of private entities or individuals. Some are only a block long, others are cul-de-sacs. Many of them are dark alleyways, but some are lined with mansions and elaborate gardens and employ security guards to keep the curious at bay. Most of us were made aware of their existence a few years ago, when out-of-town real estate speculators legally bought the common areas of high-toned Presidio Terrace at an unpaid-taxes auction. The situation turned out to have been caused by a clerical error, and the street was eventually returned to its previous owners (who have been diligent about paying their property taxes on time ever since). But the seed had been planted in acquisitive minds; similar real estate grabs continue to this day, many of them outrageous. It was my misfortune to become involved in one that turned deadly.

MONDAY, OCTOBER 31

11:35 p.m.

A light rain pattered down on the paving stones of Rowan Court, and the trees at the far end, for which the Presidio Heights court was named, shifted in a breeze. Gray clouds scudded across the dark sky. I huddled in my slicker and pulled its hood lower on my forehead. A drop of water slid down and settled on my nose.

Damn! We've had several years of drought, and when it decides to rain, it does so when I'm outside on a surveillance.

Surveillances weren't all that common for me any more. My agency was fully staffed, and I let my operatives perform the long and often tedious stakeouts. But this was Halloween, and most of my employees either were on assignment or had begged off, citing parties or the need to deal with trick-or-treaters.

I preferred to stand guard rather than deal with trick-or-treaters. Small children in outlandish costumes make me nervous. A couple of people had invited me to parties, but carving pumpkins and rowdy behavior are not my thing. Besides, my husband, Hy Ripinsky, was working a case out of our London office, so it was the job of the co-owner of

McCone & Ripinsky International to hold down the fort in his absence. My brother John was hosting a séance at his condo in SoMa, but I'd begged off that too—especially as the person he intended to bring back from the dead was Richard Nixon. Frankly, I couldn't get my spirits up—pun intended—for any of the seasonal activities. Sometime during the previous year, a curious lassitude had settled on me, and so far I hadn't been able to shake it.

What had caused the lassitude was a mystery to me. Last January I'd successfully closed a case in the extreme wilderness of northern California—Meruk County—centering on the murders of two Indigenous women that the local law had seemed inclined to dismiss. My findings had shaken the power structure there and promised vindication for many disadvantaged people. I should have been feeling satisfied, if not high, with the outcome, but instead I'd downplayed any positive emotions. Throughout the spring and summer, when asked about my sagging spirits by friends, employees, and even my husband, I'd shrugged off their questions and grimly gone about my business. As of now, nothing had changed.

Another raindrop splatted on my nose.

I was sitting on a pair of concrete steps that led up to the service entrance of the first house on the right side of the court. A coalition of the owners of the five houses on this privately owned street had hired my agency to stand guard because of recent vandalisms of various kinds—broken windows, spray-painting, damage to parked vehicles.

The house—like the others in this privileged Presidio Heights enclave—was Edwardian in style, and enormous, with red brick and dark half-timbering, many-paned windows, the lower ones protected by decorative ironwork, and a steeply peaked roof. Only security lights showed inside this one; the owners were at their winter home in Cabo San Lucas. I felt a twinge of envy, picturing sun and warm sand.

In addition to doing the Rowan Court surveillance, just this morning I'd spoken by phone with my contact there, Theresa Segretti. She'd called to say she was forming a coalition with residents of three other private streets in the city that had been similarly vandalized. Was I interested in taking them all on as clients?

Why did they want the services of my agency? I'd asked. The residents of the street were among the wealthiest in the city; they could afford to hire our best security guard services.

They weren't satisfied merely to use guards, Segretti said. In fact, many of them didn't like the presence of guards at all. What they wanted—and thought I could provide—was answers. They wanted to know why this was happening to them and who was behind it. Besides, by joining forces, they could pool their funds and hire the very best investigators the city had to offer.

I'm not above subtle flattery. And business had been slow during the past two months. I readily agreed.

She emailed me some materials on the properties and coalition members. The note she appended said the SFPD had repeatedly been contacted about the problem and presumed that the attacks on the private streets could be caused by anything from neighborhood jealousy to hatred of the elite to just plain cussedness. The police seemed to favor the latter explanation.

I wasn't so sure; four different but similar attacks on four different streets in four different parts of the city? And all of them since mid-August? I didn't think so.

In the first, at a nursery near the San Francisco Zoo, bags of fertilizer had been brought in and opened and their contents scattered around. The second had occurred on Bancroft Lane on Telegraph Hill; a fire had been set in over-grown brush next to a brick house occupied by an internet worker. The third, in an enclave called Rusty's Meadow, had involved a broken water main. And finally, Rowan Court had been spray-painted, and the owners of the properties had banded together to get to the bottom of the trouble.

No, I wasn't so sure these were random attacks.

My instincts told me there had to be a connection, but what? The vandalism could be the work of one person or a group of people. The target could be one resident of each area or all of them. So far, the residents I'd spoken with had said they knew no one on the other vandalized private streets. But still I couldn't let go of my idea that the inci-dents were somehow related.

Tomorrow, Tuesday, all my operatives would be back at the agency. We're a 24-7 operation, and the question of who's on when can become so confusing that we've posted a chart on a whiteboard in the hallway between the reception area and the offices. I'd stopped in there early this morn-ing and noted that three of my most reliable operatives—Patrick Neilan, Derek Frye, and Zoe Anderson—would be returning tomorrow. Come morning, we'd be off to a good start.

The rain slackened, but then a wind kicked up, cold and damp, soaring high off the Bay. I peered over the buildings on the downhill slope at the Golden Gate; it was shrouded in a strange, stationary fog. The horns so far had been silent, but now they began their mournful bellow.

A skittering noise in the brush beneath the rowan trees attracted my attention. I turned on my flashlight, aimed it back there. Nothing. Maybe a neighborhood cat or one of the raccoons that prowl the city seeking out garbage cans. Not a coyote, our other nocturnal type of visitor; they didn't come this close to people.

I switched off the light and leaned against the cold steps, thinking of tomorrow. I'd be free of work, and Hy wasn't due back till Wednesday. The weekend would be a good time to get an early start on Christmas shopping or catch the new exhibit at the Museum of Modern Art. Or lie lazily around the house. The latter was most appealing—

Pop!

I started. Reached automatically for my .38 in its side holster, then paused.

More popping sounds. Of course—Halloween cherry bombs. I heard a giggle as footsteps slapped around the house at the far end. Kids, not vandals. Vandals don't call attention to themselves by making unnecessary noises.

A light flared on the house's front porch. A woman stepped out, holding her dark-blue bathrobe closely around her. Theresa Segretti, the head of the neighborhood coalition and the only member I'd met with personally so far.

I stood and moved toward her, shining my light on my face so she'd know who I was.

"Ms. McCone," she called, "were those shots?"

"Just cherry bombs. Go back in the house," I said. Dammit, I'd instructed her not to come outside if there was a disturbance. Theresa—Theo—Segretti hadn't paid attention.

I ran up the wide brick steps to the door. When I stepped into the foyer, she was flattened against the wall next to the door. A small table lamp cast a semicircle on deep-piled red carpet that led up a staircase. The woman was shaking, her hands—a large diamond ring on the left—steepled against her lips, her dark hair in sweaty curls around her face.

I said to her, "It's all right. Kids playing with fireworks. I thought I told you to stay inside."

"I…couldn't. Davis is in the Far East on a buying trip, and I thought I should see what the noise was."

Davis Segretti, her husband, was an importer dealing in Asian art. I said, "That's for me to do. I'm out there by the entrance to the court. The best way you can help me is to make sure your doors and windows are locked, and turn off all lights if there's a disturbance."

"Can't you come in, sit awhile?" She motioned through an archway at a living room. The room was large, a flat-screen TV dominating the far wall, and overdecorated: wallpaper with pink and white and red blossoms against a black background; long pink velvet drapes that cascaded into heaps on the hardwood floor; flimsy little tables and spindly chairs. Except for the TV, I felt as if I'd stepped into a past century.

"Thank you, but I really should get back to my post. I do have a few questions, however. Did you see or hear anything before the fireworks went off?"

"No, nothing. But I was watching a show on Hulu, with the sound turned up."

"Have you seen anyone in the court who looked suspicious today?"

"Suspicious?"

"Like he or she didn't belong here."

"I'm not sure. I know pretty much everyone who belongs here."

"So you saw no one?"

"You're confusing me, Ms. McCone."

I'd asked a straightforward question. How could it confuse her? Then I took a close look at her eyes: they were dilated. The woman was high. Not on booze or pot; I could've smelled either, unless she'd taken an edible. Perhaps cocaine, oxycodone, or some other opioid? Maybe, but no way to tell. I didn't want to invade her privacy by asking, but I didn't like leaving her alone in this condition.

I ran through my mental file of the residents of the court: Nancy and James Knight, currently in Cabo; Emily and Chuck Carstairs, a social couple, heavily involved with the opera and museums; Jane Curry, an artist who kept mostly to herself; Marc Thomas, a photographer and gay man-about-town. None of them seemed like people I could call upon to comfort the woman.

"Mrs. Segretti," I said, "you've got to get hold of yourself. There was no real danger—just kids getting Halloween thrills. Will you be all right here tonight?"

"Yes, fine, now that you've reassured me. And my maid, Benicia Angelos, is sleeping in the servants' quarters. I'm all right now, knowing you'll be down at the gate."

"I will be. Anything you need, just reach out to me."

When I went outside, the rain had stopped completely.

Not much of a drought breaker. I returned to my perch on the cold steps. It was still two hours till my operative Zoe Anderson would relieve me.

The fog was in fully now. It's funny with fog—most of the time it's warmish and wraps you in a gentle blanket, but at other times, like this night, it's bitter cold and unfriendly. I circled my knees with my arms and curled up, my jacket's hood draped over my head like a turtle's shell.

This, I thought, is why I've expanded the agency and hired all those new operatives. This makes me remember those long, cold nights and early mornings when I was so bleary eyed after stakeouts I could barely find my car. And the tension—it was always there. The watching, the waiting. Sometimes I'd be so tense I could hardly sleep when I got home. It's spreading through me right now—

A step sounded outside the gate to the court. I started, then watched as a tall, lanky figure came toward me. I recognized its smiling face just before its arms went around me and I breathed in the familiar scent of my husband.

"Mick told me where to find you," Hy said. "Nice surprise?"

"The best. How come you're home two days early?"

"Finished up in London, so I flew to Kennedy and hitched a ride with a buddy who owns a G550. Why would I want to sit around airports when I could be in bed with you?"

TUESDAY, NOVEMBER 1

7:30 a.m.

I woke in our big bedroom at the rear of our house on Avila Street in the Marina district. Hy was still sleeping, a pillow over his head, but I'd heeded the annoying greetings of the dove that made its home in the gnarled apple tree outside the window: "Hoo, hoo hoo. Hoo, hoo hoo." Over and over.

Someday I'm going to strangle that bird.

Yeah, brave thought, McCone.

I've always been afraid of birds, something to do with a red-winged blackbird grabbing my head at our senior class picnic. I don't like the fluttering, the screeching, the flapping of feathers. Give me a fixed-wing aircraft and I'm happy.

So what to do today? Hy would sleep for hours yet, so I reached for my iPhone, checked my texts and email. Zoe reported that nothing had happened at Rowan Court during her shift and that her relief had already arrived. Most of the weekend staffers had checked in and were going about their various assignments. Derek Frye, head of our research department, had two people working their magic on the internet. Maybe I'd just stay in bed with Hy and we could—

Except the doorbell was ringing. I threw on my robe and rushed downstairs.

Ted Smalley, our office manager—"Grand Poobah," he calls himself—was standing on the steps, a FedEx envelope in his hand. His face was set in annoyed lines, and he looked as if he'd pulled his jeans and sweatshirt on over his pajamas.

"For you," he said, thrusting the envelope at me. "It was shoved through the gate at my apartment building for some reason."

"Come in," I told him. "I set the automatic percolator last night, so there's fresh coffee."

He made a huffing sound but stepped through the door. As I led him down the hallway to the kitchen, he added, "Plum Alley is my *home*, not some extension of McCone & Ripinsky. I don't know how these people got my address, anyway."

He sat down at the breakfast table, and I poured the coffee. "I don't know either. Why didn't you tell the driver to bring the mail to the office?"

"What driver? This envelope was left in the middle of the night."

"Well, you didn't have to bring it over here; it could've waited."

"I thought it might be important."

"Probably just another way of some scammer hoping to get at you or me."

I turned my attention to the envelope. There was nothing different about it from the hundred or so that live in our supply closet. My name was scrawled in big letters across the address section.

Handling it with a tissue to guard against destroying any fingerprints, I opened it. A single sheet of yellow legal paper slid out. On it, a crude map was drawn in blue ink. I turned it around, viewing it from various angles, until I could identify the location.

Bernal Heights, in the southeast part of the city. I knew it well: All Souls Legal Cooperative, where I'd worked as staff investigator for several years before starting my own agency, had been located on its lower slope near Mission Street. The weather there is among the sunniest in San Francisco, and the district is surrounded by freeways and industrial enterprises, so it seems far away from the downtown hustle and bustle.

There was nothing on the map to indicate what I should be looking for, but as I scanned it, I spotted an area of short streets that appeared to be bisected by a number of even shorter lanes. One, highlighted in yellow, caught my eye: Herrera Terrace.

I got my phone from the bedroom and checked the list of names of the city's private streets. Yes, there it was: Herrera Terrace. I googled it on Street View. Nothing. Obviously, it wasn't of enough interest to attract a photographer.

"A connection to the coalition investigation?" Ted asked.

"Maybe. Although nobody living on Herrera Terrace is a member of the group, and I doubt it's as prominent a target as the other vandalized streets. That's a rather downscale neighborhood."

"Why the map then? And why drop it off at my place rather than just mail it?"

"I'll bet that's because whoever left it knows how tight security is at the M&R building. Probably they even know how tight it is here."

"If so, I wonder how the person knows. And how they know where I live."

I shrugged. "I don't understand about not mailing it, but it's been my experience that anybody with a computer can find out anything."

Ted yawned, and I added, "Well, you've done your duty and can go back home to bed now."

He smiled wryly. "No problem. I wanted to see you anyway. It's been ages since we caught up."

I returned the smile. "That it has."

As he toyed with his coffee cup, I studied him. He looked tired. His usually neat goatee was untrimmed, and he'd lost weight.

Ted and I have been both colleagues and friends forever, since our days at All Souls Legal Cooperative. It's a solid relationship—he sheltering me through various traumas, me counseling him on his life choices. One of which was his continual alteration of his style of dress. Together we'd gone through grunge, Edwardian, Victorian, hip-hop, Hawaiian, Botany 500, ripped denim, and caftans. Under the influence of his significant other, rare-book dealer Neal Osborne (who was thoroughly sick of the wardrobe variations), he'd finally found his niche—contemporary, which is almost anything these days. Although at-home clothes thrown on over pajamas are not all that usual.

"Is everything okay with you?" I asked him.

He waggled his hand.

"What?"

"Oh, general malaise. The pandemic was tough—two gregarious people like Neal and I cooped up together. Then, when things eased, Neal was out of here like a shot."

"Out of the city? Going where?"

"Visiting friends in Australia and New Zealand. Then, since he was over there, he extended his trip to Malaysia and Singapore. Now he's in Thailand, Japan next."

"He didn't ask you to go with him?"

"In a pro forma sort of way he did. I said no—pleading work and other obligations. I didn't mention that I don't feel right about traveling on his money."

"Is that really an issue? You guys usually share everything."

"It matters to me."

I got up to fetch some more coffee. I hadn't been aware that Neal's making so much more money than Ted had become problematical for my office manager, but the stress of the pandemic had forced many couples to face up to difficulties they previously hadn't been aware of. I hoped that this time apart might ease whatever was wrong.

Ted signaled that he only wanted half a cup and said, "I guess what it is…"

"Yes?"

"It sounds so trite."

"Out with it."

"I guess what I really want is…to be married."

It wasn't an unusual desire. Since 2015, same-sex marriage had been legal in all fifty states of the union. (Although the first legal gay wedding in the country was performed at city hall in San Francisco in 2004.) Nowadays, most gay people in California have the same potential expectations and disappointments of marriage.

I said to Ted, "So what's the problem? Just propose to him."

"Kind of hard to do, since he seems determined to stay away from me as long as possible."

"You said he wanted you to go along. Fly over to Thailand or Japan and ask him to marry you. If you don't want to spend his money, a loan can be arranged for you from M&R."

"Thanks for the advice and the offer. But it just doesn't feel right."

"Why not?"

He shrugged. "Don't know. Let me think on it. We'll talk more later."

After Ted left, I studied the crudely drawn map some more, wondering who had sent it and why. The area it outlined was low income; it didn't seem to have any relationship to Rowan Court or Presidio Terrace. But it seemed obvious that the map had something to do with my investigation.

Okay, I'd take a drive over there and check it out.

I was pulling on my jeans when Hy stumbled out of the bathroom. He was barefoot, wrapped in his heavy maroon robe, with a stubbled chin and unruly hair.

"Hey," he said, blinking at me. "Where're you off to?"

"Out, for a little while."

He sat down on the bed and rubbed his eyes. "There goes the day."

"Not really, but I've got something I need to check on."

"Okay." He yawned hugely. "But keep your phone on. I may need resuscitation. This overseas travel gets harder as this old man gets older."

"You didn't act like an old man last night."

"That's because you keep me young."

9:55 a.m.

The little warren of short Bernal Heights streets clung to a rocky, badly paved hillside. Three of the houses on Herrera Terrace were squat bungalows, and a fourth looked like a failed attempt at a Gothic castle, moss furring its slate roof and crumbling brick walls. The bungalows were in equally bad repair: shingles had fallen off rooftops, exterior paint was peeling, and broken toys, tricycles, and cast-off household items littered their weedy yards. An old green Ford, circa 1980s, sat up on blocks in one driveway. I decided to try the first house, then go around the semicircle.

A little girl of maybe two or three answered my knock. "Is your mom or dad here?" I asked.

She shook her head, her whole body swaying with the movement. Then she stuck the tip of her blond ponytail in her mouth and chewed on it.

"Tanya!" An irritated voice came from behind her. "I've told you to let me answer the door!" A heavyset woman in a blue sweatshirt and faded jeans shoved her aside and peered out at me. "What?" she demanded.

"I'm looking for the owner—"

"Shit! Just try to find him."

"Maybe one of the residents of the other houses has an address or phone number?"

"Those places are squats. And for all I know the landlord's run off to Mexico with my rent check. Look at these places. Would you buy one? Or live in one if you had a choice? I'm the only person who pays rent, but can I get the landlord out here to fix things? No, I can't. Our kitchen sink's been leaking for months. Thank God for duct tape."

I said, "Have you contacted the housing authority?"

She snorted. "Government's for the haves, not people like us."

"What about People for Equitable Housing?"

"They went bust. Government here decides who gets so-called equitable treatment, and it's not us. City pulled the funding for them, threw out the director, Winslow Lambert. He raised hell, made all kinds of threats, but ended up not doing a thing."

I knew Winslow Lambert, a bombastic little man with a bulbous red nose. He was prone to shouting and throwing his considerable weight around and had a habit of taking on unpopular causes and then abandoning them when he didn't receive instantaneous popular support.

"Maybe I could help you—"

A film of hostility clouded her brown eyes. "We can take care of ourselves. Who the hell are you, anyway?"

I gave her one of my cards, and she handled it as if it might burn her fingers. After a moment she said, "You... you do stuff like that?"

"Investigations? Yes."

"Wow. Why're you here?"

"I'm looking into a series of vandalisms that have been happening on various private streets around town."

"What does that have to do with this street?"

I took out a copy of the hand-drawn map and showed it to her. She studied it, squinting. "*That's* supposed to be Herrera Terrace?"

"I think so. Has there been any vandalism in the neighborhood recently?"

"Not that I know of." She waved her hand around. "How could anybody tell if there was?"

The woman had a point. "What can you tell me about the people in the other houses?" I asked.

She came outside, closing the door behind her—presumably so Tanya wouldn't escape—and sat down on the rickety wooden stoop. I sat next to her.

"I'm Angelina," she said. "Sorry about barking at you like that; usually when somebody comes to the door here, it means trouble."

"I understand. About the other people on this block…"

"Okay," she said, pointing at the map, "this is us. Me, my old man, and Tanya. There's a couple in the next bungalow, real quiet; I don't know them. The people in the next bungalow are Jill Madison and a couple of new roommates—strangers are always dropping in there and staying awhile. Jill's okay, though. She's even got a job someplace in the Mission. Now, in that creepy place you can see down at the end, you've got Janus and Dino, both real druggies. You gotta watch out for Janus—he's stoned most of the time and gets mean when he's high. Dino, he's usually stoned too, but in a spaced-out, nonthreatening way. They've got a lot of weird people coming and going all the time, mostly at night. Customers, I guess, and pretty hardcore. Guns, you know? I don't have nothing to do with them."

A good decision—for her. We talked a little longer, but she had nothing more to tell me.

I decided to check on the quiet couple before tackling the druggies. The young woman who answered the door at their bungalow was Asian, with high-piled hair and multiple facial piercings. She looked as if she'd thrown on her robe in a hurry. When I explained who I was, she looked over her shoulder and called, "Artie!"

A lean, handsome Black man a few years older, dressed in a tank top and Levi's, appeared behind her. "What's this?"

I explained again.

"So what you're saying is, some crazy fool's gonna vandalize our street?"

"Not necessarily. Someone has been vandalizing other private streets in the city, and I've just received a map indicating yours could be next." I held out the yellow sheet.

Together they studied it. "Could be this street," the woman said.

The man—Artie—asked, "What's this with private streets, anyhow? Does that mean somebody owns Herrera Terrace?"

"Yes. A private individual or a group of some kind. I don't have any way of telling till I have time to run a title search."

"So some dude we've never heard of can just come along and yank it out from under us? Sell it and throw us all out?"

"It's not that simple. How long have you lived here?"

Artie looked at the woman. "Six months?"

"Seven. We came up here right after your mother died, remember? After she left us that five hundred dollars."

"Oh yeah, right. That five hundred went quick. We were lucky to find this place."

"Do you pay rent?" I was willing to bet they didn't.

"None of your business."

It really wasn't. "You know anything about the two guys at the end of the street?"

They exchanged glances. The woman shuddered. "Those

druggies?" she asked. When I nodded, she said, "They're real hostile. We keep as far away from them as we can."

Artie added, "Janus tried to come on to my wife once. Threatened me when I called him on it, and he wasn't just blowing smoke. After that, we gave them a wide berth."

She said, "They have knives."

"And guns?"

"I never saw a gun, but I wouldn't be surprised."

Hostility, knives, drugs, and maybe guns. Some nice neighborhood this was.

I thanked the couple for their information, gave them my card, and walked on up the street. As I went, I moved my .38 Special from my bag to the belt of my jeans. Maybe Saturday morning would be a mellow time for the two men who occupied the turreted house, but I wouldn't count on it.

The house was a real eyesore. All the windows were covered with heavy shades that would allow no light to show from within. Bramble-like vegetation grew up against the windows and crowded a narrow path to the door. Very inhospitable, unless you were a drug dealer or buyer wanting to do business in privacy.

There was an old Dodge van in the driveway but no other cars in the vicinity, so I wouldn't have any of Dino and Janus's customers or fellow druggies to deal with—just them if they were both here. I had started up the cracked front walk toward the porch when a thumping sound followed by loud voices came from a weedy side yard. I detoured in that direction.

A target—the kind archers use—was set up in the yard, grimy and beat up as if it had been salvaged from a dumpster. Something stuck out of the bull's-eye—the silver handle of a smallish knife, glinting in the sun. Two men stood side by side some twenty feet in front of the target, and as I approached, one of them made a throwing motion. I heard a whistling sound, then another thump as a second knife joined the other in the center.

"Good one, Dino!"

The man who had thrown the knife bowed to the other. He was tall, well over six feet, with close-cropped blond hair and the heavily muscled shoulders of a wrestler. His companion—shorter, black-haired, and wiry—bowed back. They heard my footsteps on the pavement at the same time and turned to look at me.

On my way over from my house in the Marina district, I'd thought up a cover story that could work in the city's current economic state, and after I'd parked I had found a generic business card in my collection to present. The collection had been created a few years back by Mick, working with different typefaces and Photoshop. Using it, I could present myself as a professional in many different occupations.

"Hey, you guys," I called to the knife throwers. "You own this property?"

Puzzled expressions. Puzzled, and wary, but not hostile—not yet, anyway.

I waved the card. "Martina Alvarez, Tri-City Real Estate. Do you have a minute?"

They made no move to examine the card, giving me long, squinty looks instead. The big one leered. I couldn't see their eyes clearly enough to tell if they were stoned, but it was a good bet that they were.

"What do you want, sweet thing?" the big one asked.

"Nice property," I said.

"No, it ain't. You blind?"

"Well, the house is certainly unique, one of a kind."

"Yeah? You want to buy it?"

"Not me. But I have a client who might be interested. Just what he's looking for."

"He must be blind too."

"Are you the owner, Mr.—?"

"Dino."

"Is that your first or last name?"

"Just Dino."

"And are you the owner, Dino?"

"No."

The wiry one, Janus, was retrieving the knives from the target. "I ain't either," he said. "We wouldn't own this dump if you give it to us."

"Why not?"

"The house is a piece of crap. The roof leaks. The plumbing's for shit. Half the time the electrical don't work."

"Who does own it?"

"Some real estate bitch." Dino leered at me again. "Not a sweet thing like you."

"What's her name?"

He took one of the knives from Janus and flung it at the target. No bull's-eye this time. "Who cares? She don't come around. Guess she's scared of us." He laughed—a strange falsetto cackling.

I asked, "How much rent does she charge you, if so much is wrong with the place?"

Janus began cleaning under his fingernails with the blade of the other knife. "Like Dino said, she don't come around."

"So then you're squatting here?"

He scowled. "What's it to you?"

"Not a thing. Half the people on this hill are squatters. Better abandoned property is put to use than allowed to deteriorate."

"You got somebody who wants to buy this dump, go hunt up the real estate bitch that owns it." There was hostility in his voice now.

"Yeah," Dino said, "the *other* real estate bitch."

Time to back off, McCone.

"I'll do that. Thanks for your time, guys."

Neither of them had anything more to say, just stood staring at me. I could feel their eyes on my back when I turned and walked around to the front of the property.

The woman who answered the door at the house where Angelina had told me Jill Madison and her friends lived was tall—close to six feet—and wore a severe black dress that reached her ankles. Her dark-brown hair was held in a knot by amber combs.

"You're the detective," she said. "Angelina called me on my cell. I'm Jill Madison. I'd ask you in, but there're… guests all over the floor. We get a lot of drop-ins stopping here on their way to someplace else."

I thought of my college days at UC Berkeley. We renters of a big, dilapidated house on Durant Avenue had had a lot of drop-ins too. A few had stayed, but most were on the move, searching for something that might be found in Hawaii or Peru or India—or anywhere else but there. The something—enlightenment, a spiritual high, or just a good time—funneled them through town and spit them out to the far corners of the earth. I wondered how many of the ones I'd known had ever found whatever they were looking for.

When I'd explained what I was after, I showed Jill the map. She gave it a cursory glance and said, "Looks like something a kindergartner might draw. But yes, I think it represents the terrace. There's been no recent vandalism here, but I wouldn't be surprised if it started up. Look, I need to get to work. You want to walk down the hill with me? We can talk on the way."

I'd left my car—a newish red Miata—near the little triangular park on Coso Avenue, across from the big brown Victorian that had once housed All Souls Legal Cooperative. Habit, I guessed. Our stroll down the slope to Mission brought back many memories: the days and nights of talking and playing cards and other games at the kitchen table in All Souls; the concrete ladder steps that gave access to sunny Bernal Heights Park, where we'd sunbathed at the very top of the hill; the Remedy Lounge, where the attorneys and support staff had spent many high, happy hours. Hank Zahn, founder of the co-op and my oldest and dearest friend from college, had been a regular. As had Ted, Jack Stewart, Anne-Marie Altman, and numerous others. We'd shared information on cases, plotted strategies, and argued politics—endless politics, from the global ("Why can't most nations get their heads screwed on straight?") to the national ("Run the assholes out of Washington!") to the state level ("More money for education, stop lining the developers' pockets!") to the local and clearly mundane ("The mayor's new hat is ugly!").

There had been many nights when I'd returned to my studio apartment several blocks away on Guerrero Street exhausted and thankful that I didn't live at All Souls, as a number of the associates did. The quiet at home, with only my cat for company, had been a welcome respite from the intensity of my days.

But those old days had been good days. Peopled by old friends, good friends. Though many were a long time gone, I cherished them all.

Jill interrupted my reminiscing by saying, "I doubt Herrera Terrace is likely to be a target of vandals, but I've read in the news about the attacks on other private streets. Who hired you?"

"A group of some of the owners."

"Which ones?"

"I'm sorry, I can't reveal that."

"Confidential, huh? Well, I can guess. The Segretti woman and her rich pals. I read on the internet that they've formed a coalition to do something about it. You're the something, right?"

"Right."

"Well, the Coalition for the Preservation of Private Streets—what a mouthful—is all well and good, but they don't seem inclined to preserve the poorer ones like mine."

"Does someone actually own this street?"

"Yes, but nobody seems interested in claiming it. We're just squatting here until whoever owns the place catches on and throws us out."

"What about the house at the end? The one with the target in the yard?"

"I don't know whose that is either. The guys there are also squatters, and pretty dangerous—guns, knives, drugs. I don't deal with them."

"Best not to."

"The thing is, titles to land here in the city are pretty hard to trace, especially the older ones, like preearthquake. A lot of the owners don't even know they own their streets. The ones who realize they do are jumping to join that coalition that hired you—if they can come up with the twenty-five hundred bucks' membership fee. It's strictly an elitist organization, in case they didn't tell you."

Jill Madison seemed quite well informed. I'd have to check her out.

I said, "So as far as you know, the attacks have all centered on wealthy neighborhoods?"

"That's all I know for sure. But considering that map that was sent to you, this neighborhood seems to be a target too. Not that I can imagine why." She paused. "If anything does happen, I'm prepared."

"How so?"

I must have looked wary, because Jill smiled and said, "No heavy-duty firepower. Just the cops and fire department on speed dial, and a couple of baseball bats. My older brothers were always afraid of me getting assaulted, and they showed me how to disable guys who annoy me."

Come to think of it, mine had too.

We'd reached Mission Street when Jill pointed to a small structure decorated to look like a cable car. "Its name is Kable Kandies," she said. "It's a cooperative. We sell healthy chocolate snacks, lollipops, brownies, butterscotch bars— all organic."

Yuck. "Do the local kids like them?"

"They do. Many of them have never had a real sweet, so they don't know the difference. Their mothers love us, and their dentists hate us." She took a candy bar from her pocket and pressed it on me.

"Thanks. Let me know if anything happens on the terrace."

"Will do."

On my way back to my car, I unwrapped the candy bar, sniffed it. Okay, it was real chocolate. I took a bite; it had a faint weedy undertaste. *Dope?* I thought hopefully and took another bite. No, just some damn healthy plant.

As I munched the chocolate bar, I thought about Jill Madison. She'd been pleasant but not terribly welcoming. And why had Angelina felt she had to notify her of my impending visit? To give her time to concoct some kind of story? About what? Jill seemed to know a great deal about the private streets. Ordinary interest, or was there something I wasn't seeing?

I reached my car, chucked the remaining chocolate bar into a convenient waste bin, and headed for the McCone & Ripinsky Building in the Financial district, where I parked in our underground garage, patting the Miata as I left it. Up until a few months ago, I'd been driving a classic Mercedes—a gift from Hy, who for years had been a classic-car junkie. But it had spent more time in the shop than it had with me, and finally I'd relinquished it to buy this cherry-red beauty. It suited me perfectly.

11:55 a.m.

Our four-story building on New Montgomery Street had been constructed in 1932 of slabs of Vermont granite. It featured the newly popular "float windows"—now termed plate glass—that permitted sunshine, moonlight, and star-shine to flood its offices and corridors. In addition to the third- and fourth-story offices, we boast several retail establishments on the lower floors, including the famous Angie's Deli, as well as a roof garden where we can relax—when the rain's not pouring down and gale-force winds aren't blowing through. Even this past summer, what with the unusual heat of the drought, we hadn't enjoyed much recreation up there.

A few years ago, we'd decided to "dress up" the building's rather staid exterior with a sculpture commissioned from the renowned Flavio St. John. When revealed—to much publicity, after Flavio had absconded to Europe with our check—it resembled a cheap concrete clamshell fused to a larger, garish gold one. A creation that Hy had proclaimed to the crowd to be "as ugly as my aunt Stella Sue's butt." (He didn't have an aunt Stella Sue, but the image has remained vivid in my memory ever since.) Fortunately, the sculpture met with a grievous "accident" weeks later and ended up in pieces in the street; among the "astonished" onlookers were Hy and my brother John.

The agency was buzzing with operatives and clients when I arrived.

Maybe business was picking up. I padded down the hallway to my office at the end of the floor and dropped my things on my armchair near the windows. The armchair, a nicely refurbished relic of my days at All Souls, sat under Mr. T., a huge schefflera plant that Ted had gifted me with when we'd moved to more stylish quarters. Then I took the stairs down a flight to our research department, where I found Derek Frye, an attractive Eurasian in his midthirties, mounted on a many-wheeled instrument of torture, pedaling furiously while watching CNN on a screen mounted on its handlebars. I watched him enviously; he was barely sweating.

When he saw me come into his office, he jumped off the contraption. "Shar! How's it going?"

I shrugged, pointed at the screen. "Anything interesting?"

"Just the usual shit. Sometimes I wonder why I bother to watch."

"Know what you mean."

He grabbed a towel and ran it over his face and the tasteful tattoo of linked snakes that circled his neck. "I sent you the data you requested yesterday on the history of those private streets. Their owners too. There wasn't much on most of them, but I culled out the interesting ones."

Derek Frye was a technological wizard and one of my best operatives. He'd come to the agency straight out of Stanford and in a couple of years had revamped our computer and security systems, plus found time to establish one of the best real-time websites of its day, SavageFor, in partnership with my nephew, Mick Savage. They'd soon sold out to an internet giant called Omnivore, and though it would have been easy for both of them—having been born into wealth—to give in to frivolous pursuits, they'd continued to investigate and bring innovative designs to our databases. Derek, in particular, had good reason to pursue his chosen career: his father, Martin Frye, a domineering man who had made his fortune in a nationwide chain of grocery stores, had made a will leaving the bulk of his estate in trust for his son, with the stipulation that he work in "a meaningful occupation" until the age of forty-five. Derek had confided to me that his father didn't admire his work and often ridiculed it as "ludicrous" but allowed it since it technically fit the definition set forth in the trust.

Now Derek grinned at me and asked what I needed. I gave him a list, including Jill Madison, Dino, Janus, and the turreted house at the end of Herrera Terrace. He said he'd have a full battery of what I'd asked for by close of business. Then I went upstairs to go over the files on the private streets again, this time concentrating on their history.

In my office, I sat at the computer to access Derek's file on the private-street owners.

It was large, but he'd bulleted the names that he considered important. As I clicked through them, I was surprised. Two highly placed city government officials. Three society women who were frequently photographed in what were, to my taste, ridiculous gowns at openings of the opera and ballet. An author who was yearly pissed off when he didn't win the Pulitzer Prize. A celebrity chef. A pundit whose columns ran irregularly in the *Chronicle*. An internet persona who identified himself as Sam-the-Sage.

Which ones could I get interviews with? Neither of the politicians—I'd tangled with both before. One of the society people who actually cared about the city—rich and poor alike? Maybe. The pissed-off writer? Possibly. I'd heard he loved an audience. The pundit? No, too self-important. The chef? No, too busy producing his daily TV show. And then there was Sam Sage....

I knew Sam Sage from way back. He'd once been a member of our local mime troupe. Then he'd gone to New York, where he'd appeared in a few off-Broadway productions. Upon returning to the city, for a time he'd eked out a living as a model for mail-order catalogs. I'd heard a rumor that he was involved in porn films, but for the last few years he'd confined himself to the internet, largely refuting whatever claims otherwise sensible people made there. He grandiosely referred to himself as an "influencer"—a term usually referring to marketing people who were paid to steer followers to products and services. Just what products and services Sam might be trying to provide was unclear, but he must be earning a living because he lived in a fairly upscale neighborhood. His private street was called Bancroft Lane, on the western side of Russian Hill. It had been the second to be vandalized.

I decided to check out his home.

12:40 p.m.

Bancroft Lane was narrow, its pavement potholed in places—more of a trail than a street. Dead branches and blackberry vines crowded in on both sides. Glad I'd left my pretty car down on Greenwich, I hiked up through the brittle vegetation. Three smallish brick dwellings, none of them currently inhabited according to Derek's report, were strung along the right side of the trail. Halfway up I spotted a sedan nosed into a thicket on the opposite side. It was light colored and long, with the high tail fins associated with the late fifties or early sixties. Scattered around it were rusted appliances and broken-down furniture—an urban dumping ground. Past that I found myself in a clearing, facing an ivy-covered brick wall with verdigris cupolas at its corners. A battered white Toyota truck was pulled up next to it, and a dirt path led around the left side. I followed it.

The brick building reminded me of a miniature fort, with two small barred windows and a similarly fortified door; a tarnished brass bell was suspended on a hook beside the door, with a hammer attached by a chain and a sign reading PLEASE RING. A giant satellite dish on the flat roof was its only present-day amenity. I pounded on the bell with the hammer.

"All right, all right!" The voice from inside sounded testy. "I'm coming. You don't have to knock the place down!"

The door creaked open on rusty hinges, and Sam-the-Sage peered out. In the three or four years since I'd last seen him, he seemed to have grown a foot shorter, ten years older, and completely bald. I blinked in surprise, and so did he. Then he said, "Well, if it isn't Superdick herself."

I'd heard that was his internet name for me, and I was not amused.

"Sammy," I said, "how you doin'?"

He grunted in annoyance. "I suppose you're here about the private-streets coalition."

"Yes. May I come in?"

Ungraciously he stepped back and threw the door open.

Inside, the place was dim and smelled of dope. The walls were brick like the outside, and a welter of mismatched furniture was set against them so the center of the room could accommodate an oversize yoga mat.

Sam said, "Sit."

I selected the most comfortable-looking sofa, a faded orange flowered thing. Dust puffed up from it.

Sam sat on the mat and assumed the lotus position. "So what do you want to know?"

"Let's start with the fire that damaged the other buildings up here. When did that happen?"

"Last August."

I'd read accounts of the fire but wanted to quiz Sam in case he had additional information. "Go on."

"It started late at night, burned very fast; the grounds hadn't been kept up, and there were a lot of weeds. The fire department put it out before it spread and caused any real damage."

"Were the buildings occupied?"

"No. Not for some time. There'd been a change of ownership, and the others left because of a rent increase."

"Who owns the houses?"

"Some damn corporation. I don't concern myself with them."

"How did the fire start?"

He shrugged. "It was dismissed as 'cause undetermined.'"

"Do the police have files on the incident?"

"'The incident.' God, do you sound establishment. Of course, you've come a long way since the legal co-op. Got yourself a big agency now, a building downtown, a house in the Marina, an airplane, even a husband. Doin' good, McCone."

I was, but the things he'd mentioned—save for Hy—were only the trappings of success. What mattered to me was that I still cared about my clients, fought hard for them, and in most cases discovered the truth. Same as I had when I worked for a rock-bottom salary out of a coat closet under the stairs at All Souls.

I turned the conversation back in the right direction. "So the fire made you decide to become a member of the coalition?"

"A member? I *founded* it. In a way, I *am* the coalition,

given how little work the others do. Of course, their money is a consideration."

Sam had founded the coalition? Theo Segretti hadn't told me that. Why not, if it was true? I said, "I thought Theresa Segretti was the founder."

He scowled. "Oh, she's always trying to take credit for things she didn't do. Always wants to be in charge."

"So you don't like the woman."

"Never mind about her. Listen, I'm busy. Let's get this interview over with."

"Just a few more questions. What's the coalition's mission statement? Why was it established? What's it supposed to do?"

"'Mission statement'? Listen to you—you sound like a lawyer. It's to keep outsiders from messing with the private streets. Prevent higher city taxes. Stuff like that."

"I understand there's a hefty membership fee. What is that used for?"

He shrugged again. "Printing costs—we put out a newsletter and lots of posters and flyers. Office rental, phone, supplies, internet connection, copying fees, electricity, garbage, water and sewer, insurance—all the usual crap."

I hadn't seen any of those posters or newsletters, but they weren't the sort of thing that would attract my attention. "So this is the office, as well as your home?"

"Right. Everything's done out of here."

"What about support staff?"

"The staff is all volunteer."

"Accountants' or attorneys' fees?"

He was looking irritated now. "Also volunteers."

"So you must file as a nonprofit with the IRS."

"...I leave all that shit up to the experts."

"You mind telling me who they are?"

"Yes, I do! You've got no right coming in here and asking me this stuff. You forget—I'm your employer."

"Technically the coalition is."

"You don't need all that stuff from me to find out who's been trashing our streets."

"I require extensive background information on my clients."

"Well, you're not getting it from me!" His face flushed, and he stood, fists balled at his sides. I stood too. There was no point in goading him any more. "Thank you for your time, Sam." I put out my hand, but he ignored it.

As I let myself out, I decided to ask my own lawyer my questions.

1:55 p.m.

I'd known Hank Zahn since we were residents of the big Durant Avenue house in Berkeley. He'd been in law school then; I'd been a sociology major scraping together tuition in security work. When he established All Souls—a cooperative providing its clients with legal aid on a sliding scale according to their ability to pay—he'd hired me as their private investigator.

A lot had changed since then. Hank had married Anne-Marie Altman, another of the co-op's attorneys, and, when the group split up, they'd established their own firm. They'd bought a two-flat house in the Noe Valley district—separate flats because their personal habits were incompatible. They'd adopted a daughter, Habiba Hamid, who'd divided her time between the flats. Eventually they'd divorced, and Anne-Marie had taken a dream job in Dallas. Habiba had insisted on remaining in San Francisco, though she visited her mom frequently. And Hank remained in the house, working out of the lower flat.

I found him this afternoon in his office at the front of the ground floor, slouched in his chair with his feet on the desk, frowning in concentration. "Am I interrupting?" I asked.

"Shar! No, I was just trying to decide whether to cook or order pizza for dinner."

"Heavy thoughts—pun intended."

"Sit down, take a load off—pun also intended."

I sat.

"So, what's up?" he asked.

"I need information on a nonprofit organization." I explained about the coalition.

"What kind of information?"

"Anything you can lay hand to."

He made a few notes on his desktop computer. "How soon do you need it?"

"ASAP."

"Figures. Let me check on a few things while you're here." He busied himself at the keyboard.

I looked around the small office. Its walls were lined with barrister bookcases; papers and files were piled on the floor and the tops of cabinets; his politically incorrect cigar-store Indian guarded two stacks of newspapers. There would be more newspapers in other rooms. Hank is an information junkie and prefers it in print; he subscribes to about seven dailies and four Sunday editions. His horn-rimmed glasses look thicker to me these days—small wonder. He hit a button, and somewhere behind the newspapers a printer whirred.

"The coalition's a nonprofit, all right," he said, swiveling and running his fingers through his wiry gray hair. "I'm printing out what's available in the public record. So how's by you?"

"All's good. Hy was in London; now he's home. I'm hoping he'll stick around for a while. How's Habiba?"

"She's thirteen."

"A hellion, huh?"

"It's not a pretty age. The latest is she wants me to live down here so she can have the whole upper flat to herself."

"Why?"

"Sex parties? Witchcraft? Cannibalism? Who knows? Like I said, she's thirteen. I may survive to see her turn twenty-one." He didn't look particularly upset, though.

"You're an easygoing dad."

"I am, till the going gets tough. Then she'd better watch out."

The printer stopped whirring. Hank got up and fetched a handful of paper. "Here. Why don't you look at these, and then we'll discuss them. I'll get us some wine."

What he'd printed out was mainly forms: state form CT-1, registration certificate for charity trusts, annual certificates of renewal, certified articles of incorporation, organization's current bylaws, IRS determination letter, application for recognition of tax exemption from the IRS. I skimmed them. Sam's claim that he was the founder of the organization was not reflected in any of them. They were all signed by Theresa Segretti.

Hank appeared with two glasses of wine and a half-full bottle: Deer Hill Chardonnay, my favorite. We settled down, sipping, and he said, "Those docs make any sense to you?"

"More or less."

"Overall, what they show is that the coalition has complied with all the requirements for status as a nonprofit in this state. They were prepared by an attorney whom I know, and I can check with her to see if there were any irregularities or difficulties."

"Would she tell you if there were?"

"She'd tell me; we go a long way back." He wiggled his bushy eyebrows suggestively.

"Anyone I know?"

"She was before your time. Let me see if I can reach her now." He hit his speed dial, waited, then said, "Hey, Jenny, it's Hank. Is the supreme leader in? No? Well, please ask her to give me a call when it's convenient." He added to me as he hung up, "Jenny's a ditz; she'll forget to write down the message, and I'll have to call back."

"While we wait, there's something else I want to ask you: What do you know about private streets here in the city?"

"Well, there're a lot of them, and some go back to the nineteenth century. Titles are cloudy, taxes go unpaid. The city doesn't work to straighten out the situation—something about not wanting to take them over and become a landlord. Frankly, I think it's due more to our famous bureaucratic laziness than anything else."

"So in a lot of cases nobody knows or cares who the rightful owners are?"

"That's about it."

"Seems strange in a city that's as real estate hungry as San Francisco."

"Well, booms and busts have come and gone. When the city—Yerba Buena, it was called—was first settled, people took to the hills and built mansions with their Gold Country fortunes. Then came the quake of '06, and survivors pushed out above Van Ness Avenue and into the Richmond and Sunset districts. In the thirties, the developer Henry Doelger created those cookie-cutter houses in the southern areas, and they became very popular with the GIs returning from both World Wars. The real estate value under all those buildings has changed drastically according to time and tastes."

"So what's the latest big thing?"

Hank considered, frowning. "Luxury, mostly in condominium complexes. There isn't much available land in desirable areas, so developers are being forced to build up."

"So it would seem that the undesirable areas of the city are becoming more valuable."

"That's the way it works. If you like, I can show you some charts and tables."

There was nothing I would have liked less than a Hank Zahn presentation of charts and tables. When he got wound up on a subject, his audience often came away with volumes of answers to what was basically a simple question.

I looked at my watch. "Oh, I'm sorry." It was almost three; time goes by swiftly when you're navigating the congested city streets and trying to find parking spaces. "I've got an appointment across town, so I better get going. Let me know if your friend says anything about irregularities with the coalition."

4:25 p.m.

FlorArt was on a privately owned street called Maynard
Way off Sloat Boulevard, near the zoo and the Great Highway. The shop was a tiny, brown-shingled building on the
corner. Redwood flower boxes sat on the sidewalk, and the
tops of young trees peeked over its fences. As I approached,
I could smell jasmine; the planters were filled with pansies.
Inside the office were shelves displaying an assortment of
vases, plant food, and small bags of potting soil. No one
was in the office, so I went through to the back, where
camellia bushes and Japanese maples rose against a line of
fir trees.

A woman called from the rear, "Please come in. You're
Ms. McCone, I'll bet." Her round face was rosy from the
cold, her body encased in a heavy fleece jacket and leggings.
She pulled off dirt-encrusted gardening gloves before shaking my hand.

"I'm Carol Collins," she told me. "Oh, what am I saying?
You know that. Come inside where it's warm."

Behind a row of decorative pots was a small seating
area—two easy chairs and an electric fireplace that glowed
red hot. "I don't know about you," Carol Collins said, "but I
could do with a snort of brandy right now."

"Sounds good."

When we'd settled into the chairs with thick tumblers in
hand—more than a snort, that was for sure—I said, "You
know that the Coalition for the Preservation of Private
Streets has hired me to look into the vandalism trouble."

"Sure do. I was one of the main ones lobbying for you."

"I understand this was the first street to be attacked."

Although I was familiar with what had happened, I wanted to hear it in Collins's own words.

"You bet it was—with shit. Suckers dragged in bags of fertilizer and spread it all over the place."

"You say 'suckers'—plural. Could it have been the work of one person?"

"Well, it was the middle of the night. One person could've had plenty of time to do his, er, dirty work." She grinned wickedly.

"And nobody realized what was going on?"

"The five places here are mainly businesses. None of the owners live on-site except for Bernie and me. My living quarters are at the rear, so I really can't hear much. Bernie was away when it happened; she's a pilot for Southwest, gone a lot."

"You called the police?"

"Yeah. They seemed to think it was funny."

I'd have an operative ask them for a report, see how funny they thought that was.

"What happened to the fertilizer?"

"A friend of mine's a landscaper. He salvaged what he could and took it as payment, hosed down the rest. Plants here are gonna be going wild this coming spring."

"Have you received any communication about what happened? Notes, emails, phone calls?"

"None."

"Has anyone on the street had serious disagreements with someone else?"

"No. We're friendly, all keep in touch with each other. I take care of Bernie's cat, Jasper, when she's gone."

It was well after five thirty by now. I drained my glass

and said, "I'll stop by tomorrow to talk with the other shopkeepers."

"Thank you for your attention to this problem, Ms. McCone."

"Not to worry. I'll find out what's going on."

7:00 p.m.

Edmund Spenser, another coalition member, was having a signing for his new book, *Just You and Me, Darlin'*, at a small neighborhood store in the Haight. Stores like this, the Intrepid Reader, are going out of business across the country; the proliferation of big chain bookstores started it, and the lure of ordering by computer for next-day delivery is what's responsible now. Only devoted customers and authors keep them hanging on. I myself love the Intrepid Reader: its extensive shelving where you can search for books on any subject, its well-informed and helpful staff, its labyrinths and cozy nooks where you can curl up in an old armchair to sample the wares.

Tonight the main floor was cleared of displays, and rows of folding chairs had been set up. A number of people sat there, looking attentive; a couple had pads and pencils in hand. Were they reporters? Aspiring authors? Or people who felt it necessary to document the passage of their days?

Edmund Spenser was already seated at the speaker's table, flanked by two stacks of his new book. He was lean, with carefully styled gray hair, dressed in what I think of as the standard professorial uniform—tweed jacket with suede elbow patches, chinos, and boots. As I seated myself in the back row, he was answering a question from the audience.

"Fiction does not mirror real life. It *is* real life. At least more than any of us experience it."

Huh?

"I wouldn't say that any of my characters are reflective of my life. But then I wouldn't say they aren't."

So which is it?

"Fiction now? It's healthy. I have to say that I myself am writing some of the best damn fiction on the planet."

Hearing that, I slipped out of my seat and went back to the bookshop's office, where I found the owner, Maggie Wolfson.

"You're skipping out?" she said.

"Not really. I need to interview your speaker."

"What's he done? Other than bore about thirty of my best customers?"

"Actually, he's a client. Can you hold him here when the people go?"

"Shouldn't be a problem. They've been sneaking out one by one. Except for the gentleman sleeping in the back row."

I looked where she pointed. The "gentleman" in tattered clothing appeared to be a homeless person who had wandered in to get out of the cold.

"What do you do about people like that?"

"Let them rest. And when we close, there's a heated shed for them in the alley."

Edmund Spenser droned on for another fifteen minutes while I browsed in the cookbook section, looking for a Christmas gift for my friend Jane. Words and phrases filtered through from the other room: *literary paradigm*; *allusion*; *paraleipsis*; *epigraph*. I shuddered, thinking of the

English lit classes that had been required in college. Reading I enjoy; technical terms I do not.

When I heard chairs scraping and footsteps heading for the door, I returned to the office, where Edmund Spenser greeted me cordially. "Ms. McCone, so you're the investigator we've hired. I expected you'd be contacting me."

"Good to meet you. Is there somewhere we can talk privately?"

He looked at his watch. "The café closes at nine. Will that be enough time?"

We went to the bookshop café—a trapping that made its way into the retail environment in the 1990s and has since become de rigueur. There, amid the odors of coffee and muffins and cinnamon, we talked.

Edmund Spenser's four-house private street, Rusty's Meadow, had been the third place to be attacked. It was situated in the South of Market district, overlooking the Embarcadero and South Beach Harbor. "We have beautiful views and very little traffic, including pedestrian," Spenser said. "Which is why this incursion is so upsetting."

"Describe the incursion."

"A month ago, a water main ruptured. At least, that's what my neighbors and I thought. The ground floors of our homes were flooded, plantings were washed away, a couple of vehicles parked at the curb were damaged. When the city inspectors came out, they said there was evidence that the main had been deliberately tampered with. I've called and called but can get no satisfaction about how their investigation is proceeding. My insurance company's had no luck either; they can't settle my claim until they get some answers."

"Did the flooding do much damage?"

"Destroyed all but one of my Persian rugs. The same for some books on the lower shelves. The hardwood floors are still a mess. I can't afford to do anything until my claim can be settled."

I made a mental note to have one of the operatives talk to the city investigators and Spenser's insurance company.

"What about your neighbors?" I asked. "Have they had similar difficulties?"

"Oh yes. Gloria next door didn't even have insurance, so she's sunk. The Allens up the block had the least damage and have had it repaired. The old man across from me, Jim Ridley, was devastated. I talked to his niece the other day; they're moving him to a home in San Mateo and selling the house."

"I'd like to have my operatives speak to the others, if I could. And take a look at the street."

Spenser nodded and noted down addresses and phone numbers of the people on his street—as well as the numbers of his insurance agent and the city inspector. "I'll be at home all day tomorrow, so stop by—no need to call first."

A young, timid-looking woman came into the café, clutching one of his books. "Mr. Spenser," she said, "I was late for your talk, but would you sign my copy?"

"I'd be glad to."

I waved goodbye and got out of there.

9:32 p.m.

Hy and I brainstormed over his wonderful stew and polenta. He's a good cook, specializing in Italian dishes, and seldom uses recipes, knowing instinctively what will work with what. The only failure I can remember came when he bought what was labeled as a roasting chicken but turned out to be a stringy old stewing hen. We roasted it but couldn't pierce the skin to get to the meat.

"Could whoever's behind the vandalism be an insider?" he asked. "Someone who wants to capitalize on the publicity?"

"Not such great publicity, is it? Not if these incidents are designed to force the sale of houses. I'd say the publicity would be a deterrent."

"Yeah. Imagine shelling out what it costs for a single-family house in this city and then getting attacked by vandals."

I thought of my former home on the tail end of Church in the Glen Park district. It had been burned to the ground by a vandal—someone who didn't like the way I'd handled a case he'd hired me to solve. I'd almost lost my life and two cats in that fire, and I had lost my car, furnishings, and keepsakes and all my valuables that hadn't been stored in the US Navy ammunition box I'd kept bolted to the floor in one closet. Arson was one of the crimes I feared and hated the most.

Hy said, "Could the vandal be an enemy, then? Someone holding a grudge?"

"An enemy of people on all the streets? Derek's had people looking for connections, and there don't seem to be any."

"A speculator, trying to lower property values in order to buy up the land?"

"Rumors about real estate are always rife, you know, but none of our people has heard of anyone with such plans."

"So the perps just like to hit and destroy?"

I shook my head. "I don't think it's that random."

"Your famous gut instinct, right?"

"Uh-huh. And speaking of that—is there any more of that polenta?"

He laughed and passed the dish over. As I ladled it onto my plate, I thought how lucky I was to have found him. All the men I'd been involved with before paled in comparison.

I'd had the usual high school boyfriends, some more serious than others, plus an older man I'd thought I was in love with before I'd come to my senses. College hadn't provided much time for developing relationships, what with my heavy work and study schedules. I suppose that accounted for my later dismal record with men.

The memory of the first of those usually makes me cringe. Lieutenant Gregory Marcus of the city's homicide detail had been handsome, instructive about techniques of investigation, and loving—but with a fatal flaw: he persisted in calling me "Papoose" in honor—*he* thought—of my dark Native looks. When we'd broken up, we'd remained friends; he was now growing oranges on his ranch in the Gold Country.

No one had been memorable after Greg until Don DelBoccio.

Don had been a disc jockey on the loudest, most annoying radio station in town. When we'd met, I'd found him not at all annoying; he was a scholar, a graduate of the Eastman School of Music in Rochester, New York. Our relationship, however, had become tepid, and we'd scrapped plans to move in together. Don had remained the scourge of the airways, although I sometimes visited his apartment in a converted loft south of Market to share wine and listen to his favorite classics.

Finally, I'd almost made what would have been the worst mistake of my life: George Kostakos, professor of psychology at Stanford University. A young man, Bobby Foster, had been convicted and sentenced to death for the murder of George's missing daughter, Tracy—a rare "no body" case in which there was no physical evidence that a murder had been committed. I'd been hired by a prisoners' advocacy group to prove Foster's innocence—which I had, as well as locating the young woman's grave—and in the course of my investigation had become involved with her bereaved father. Later he'd asked me to move in with him, the implication being that we'd eventually marry and have a child to replace the daughter he'd lost.

The proposal didn't feel right to me, and I fled. Fled northeast to the volcanic fields around Tufa Lake in Mono County, where Hy Ripinsky, whom I'd met on a case the previous summer, had a small ranch. In spite of my having given him no warning, when Hy opened his door and saw me standing there, he'd said, "It's about time, McCone," and ushered me inside. We'd discovered then that we shared an unusual psychic connection that has served us well ever since. Later, on one of our frequent flights between Mono County and the Bay Area, he'd asked me to marry him. I was caught totally off guard, and when I said yes, he immediately changed our flight path toward Reno—before, as he put it, I could change my mind.

I never would have considered it.

Now he said, "Let's leave the dishes for morning. I've got plans for us."

WEDNESDAY, NOVEMBER 2

8:30 a.m.

The morning was gray, with gravid clouds threatening more rain. Our cats, Alex and Jessie, were spooked by the atmospheric changes; they huddled together on the kitchen windowsill, looking out warily. Even the dove was silent; he was in his apple tree, and only a few rustlings betrayed him.

Hy was talking on the phone to somebody in Denver.

I studied him. Tall and rangy, with dark-blond hair, he has keen brown eyes and a prominent hawk nose above a bushy mustache and full lips. Not classically handsome, but definitely attractive, as attested to by the admiring gazes I'd observed from women when they spotted him. Finally he hung up and said he might have to fly to Colorado today if the situation worsened.

What situation? I asked him.

"Kid with a gun," he said. "Possible hostage taking brewing."

Hy was good at talking desperate people down, and he had been getting plenty of practice at it recently, as it seemed we were producing more and more crazies immune to reason. He'd learned his negotiating skills from various activities: as a pilot in Southeast Asia ferrying embattled citizens from their war-torn countries to safety, as an environmental activist protesting the potential destruction of national treasures, and later as a security specialist in the executive protection field. His calm, empathetic manner had brought many a crisis to a successful resolution. I responded to this latest situation with my own brand of calm, and to take my mind off my uneasiness, I asked him to be in touch soonest. Then I drove to the McCone & Ripinsky Building.

Before I went to my office, I stopped in at Derek's and asked him if he'd gather additional information on Jill Madison, Dino, and Janus. He said he'd have it by close of business. Then I went to my office and studied the file he'd sent on the private streets.

Rowan Court: Its homes had been built in the brief Edwardian era (1901 to 1910) after the mining and lumber barons had claimed their exalted perches atop nearby Nob Hill. All five houses had belonged to those of the elite merchant class: shopkeepers glorified as purveyors of fine art, antiquities, and jewelry. While no Magnins or Gumps lived there today, some of the residents were descendants of those entrepreneurs. In the 1880s, roving bands of vigilantes had taken over the land and had been rousted by the residents, but since 1910, there had been no outstanding events in the court, except for elaborate weddings and funerals.

Bancroft Lane: Settled in the 1910s by members of the Bancroft family, who had acquired the Bancroft Library at my alma mater, UC Berkeley, in the early 1900s. The buildings in San Francisco had been inhabited by the Bancrofts for only two decades, then left in the hands of real estate brokers who never managed to sell the entire parcel. Those homes that had been purchased turned over rapidly; former owners contended the place was haunted. Bancroft's ghost?

Enough with the puns, McCone.

Maynard Way: As Carol Collins had told me, the street had been mostly commercial since its establishment in the mid-1920s as an adjunct to the Zoological Gardens and Fleishhacker Playfield. The zoo was the only remainder of the pleasurable attractions of the era. Fleishhacker Pool, a tank that contained over six million gallons of warm salt water, was long gone. The Playfield, with its miniature railroad and donkey rides, turned into the amusement park called Playland-at-the-Beach and was then leveled in the 1970s for a condominium complex. Farther up the Great Highway, the venerable Cliff House had assumed various identities.

Rusty's Meadow: An oddity, perched high above the great piers of the Embarcadero, where the atmosphere of the old waterfront clung perilously in the remaining saloons, cafés, stores, and tattoo parlors. It was once a bucolic knob where residents raised sheep and cattle. Rusty, for whom the meadow was named, was a retired circus horse who performed tricks for neighborhood children until his demise in 1902. Low-income housing now proliferates on the lower slope, except for the wealthy enclave of condominiums at the tip of the knob, formerly named after Marvin Koslowski, a settler from Poland, who purchased much of the land in 1899. The acreage was eventually sold off as the family's fortunes declined.

Herrera Terrace wasn't one of the coalition streets, but

the map that had been sent to me warranted its inclusion, and Derek had supplied the information about it that I'd asked for. It had been a working-class neighborhood. Its settlers had been seamen, laborers, and ordinary shopkeepers. The population had changed from decade to decade due to the influxes of new industries and war workers. Longshoremen, shipbuilders, machinists, and wharf builders swelled the number of residents on the heights after the 1906 quake, and waterfront skirmishes between organized labor and scabs were common; in July of 1934 a battle was fought between strikers and the police, culminating on the legendary "Bloody Thursday." Labor disputes after the start of World War II were rare, and management and the workers who lived on the heights came to an uneasy truce. Beginning in the early 2000s, a large influx of middle-class families with children had gentrified parts of the hill, and they were now considered a highly desirable place to live.

So what did I have? A greater grasp of local history, but no greater understanding of what linked the attacks or what connection Herrera Terrace had to the vandalized streets.

Maybe they weren't all linked? Or were linked in a different way from what I'd been speculating? Maybe... Oh, hell!

It was almost noon, and I was hungry. I collected my nephew Mick and took him down the block to a new Peruvian restaurant that had just opened up.

Mick Savage had joined forces with me several years before, when he'd been sent north by my sister Charlene and her then-husband Ricky Savage. A disgraceful episode involving Mick hacking into the mainframe of the Pacific Palisades Board of Education and collecting information on teachers and students—presumably to use for his own wicked purposes—had resulted in his expulsion, and he'd been sent to Aunt Sharon so she could shape him up. Just why they'd considered me a person who could force their wayward son to toe the line has always been a mystery to me; what I *had* done was turn him into a private investigator.

He'd become a good one. He was tall and slightly overweight, blond like his mother and handsome like his father, and his boyish good looks fooled people into thinking nothing wily could be going on behind his innocent façade. Not so, however; the wheels of speculation and suspicion were always turning.

For years we'd played a game in which I'd exchange his special help on matters not strictly in his purview for meals at restaurants of his choice (limited to the Bay Area). Now, at our window table at La Mar Cebichería Peruana, he dug into his steak with anticuchera sauce with gusto while I toyed with my ahi and told him about the private-streets case.

"I've loaded Derek up with background work," I said. "Can I count on you to fill in on anything else that might come up?"

"Sure thing," he told me, signaling for another round of drinks. "I've got all the time in the world these days."

I studied him. Lately he'd been busy with the new house he'd bought on Telegraph Hill near Coit Tower—decorating and setting up a home office. He hadn't mentioned any women, and I was pretty sure he hadn't been seeing anybody in a long time. But I didn't ask; there were boundaries in our relationship that I didn't cross, and that was one of them.

All I said was, "I'm glad I can depend on you."

1:46 p.m.

I'd decided to devote the afternoon to exploring the private streets that I hadn't taken a very good look at so far. Starting with the shops on Maynard Way, near the zoo.

The businesses there were an assorted group. Besides Carol Collins's FlorArt, there were Old Shanghai (Chinese curio and tea shop), Mel's Fleet Feet (athletic footwear), the Silversmith (fine jewelry by appointment), and a vacant storefront below the apartment where the airline pilot Bernie Hebart and her cat, Jasper, lived.

Old Shanghai was a place where cheap old souvenirs went to languish. The young man behind the counter had—or pretended to have—very little English and kept steering me to a display of ugly teapots. I bought some jasmine tea to make him feel good.

An athletic-looking blond woman at Fleet Feet asked me how many miles a day I ran, and when I lied and told her five, she drifted away, unimpressed. A sign in the Silversmith's window told me to make an appointment. Bernie Hebart wasn't home, and the cat, Jasper, didn't answer my summons.

3:10 p.m.

Okay, Edmund Spenser had invited me to stop by his Rusty's Meadow residence anytime; he'd be home all day. I called to make sure and then drove up there, admiring the wide vistas of the waterfront and bay and contrasting them to the squalor of the hillside neighborhood. The public housing projects down there were two-story dirty-beige buildings with small windows facing other small windows on opposing wings. The common areas had gone to weeds, and the only play equipment was a swing set minus seats and a broken teeter-totter. The hill had once been forested with oak trees, but it looked as if a giant chain saw had swept through and toppled them.

The high gates in a fence that circled the very top of the knoll were another study in contrasts to the public housing: no chain link and metal piping here. The gates were of some alloy that mimicked brass, and across them RUSTY's MEADOW was spelled in ornate letters. A discreet guardhouse was tucked to one side, and a uniformed woman came out.

"Ms. McCone?" she asked. "To see Mr. Spenser?"

"Yes."

"He had to go out on an errand, but he asked that I admit you. You can park in his driveway—it's number four, up the curve to your right—and he'll join you in ten minutes or so."

I thanked her, turned to the right, and pulled up in the circular drive of a low-slung house of natural stone and pine that was cantilevered over a slope that fell away to the remains of the shipyards. The slope was rugged and peppered with loose stones and broken concrete and rusted construction equipment. Spenser, as he'd claimed, had a great view—if you didn't look straight down.

The rain I'd been expecting all day had started. First sprinkles and then larger drops. After a bit the interior of the car began to steam up. I looked at my watch; more than fifteen minutes had passed. Where was Spenser? I opened my window, breathing in the good smells of fresh, damp air, took my red slicker from where I always kept it stashed behind the seat, got out, and put it on. Moved around the side of house toward the cliff face to take a better look at the Embarcadero.

A car was coming uphill toward the gate at a fast pace. As it entered, I turned to see if it was Spenser's. It was black, coated in rain-splattered dust. Some sort of luxury model—

Suddenly it veered and came straight at me.

I scrambled backward and to one side. The car kept coming. I dodged onto the edge of the hillside, and the muddy ground crumbled beneath my feet. The front bumper of the car narrowly missed me. I slid to my knees, the earth giving way under me so that I had no chance to get back onto solid ground. All I could do was tuck and roll when I began sliding down the slope.

I slammed face down onto the gravel; my hands slipped when I tried to gain purchase. Pain seared my shoulder and ribs, and at some point I flipped over onto my back hard enough to take my breath away. Then something big and solid ended my fall; I lay against whatever it was, unable to move. The pain continued in waves, making me shudder from head to toe. The rain splattered down harder; I licked the drops from my lips.

Scrabbling sounds from above. Somebody scrambling down. And the car—where was it? I tried to look up, groaned in protest.

"Don't move," said the voice of the woman from the guardhouse. "Lie still till we can see what we've got here."

"...I...a car..."

"I know. I was coming back from a restroom break when I saw you fall. Don't move!" Hands touched me gently here and there. Then, "Doesn't look like you have any serious injuries, but I can't be sure. I'm going to call 911."

I felt disoriented from the pain in my head and my ribs. I tried to sit up, decided against it. I brushed the muddy wetness from my face, tried to breathe deeply, stopped when that also seemed like a bad idea. The big thing I'd come to a stop against seemed to be a smooth boulder. I hitched myself up against it until breathing was easier.

I was shivering from the wet and cold as I waited. Soon there were more scrabbling noises from above. A team of EMTs—a man and a woman—checked me over, told me I probably had no broken bones. Then they carried me carefully up the steep slope on a stretcher, pain throbbing throughout my head and body, and put me into an ambulance.

"Give me one of those blankets," the male EMT said. He tucked it around me, then wiped my wet face and smoothed back my hair.

The wheels rumbled on the pavement. I wanted to ask where they were taking me but could only come out with a garbled syllable. For a while I lost track of time, knowing only that I was warm and dry. Then the ambulance stopped, and I was wheeled into a brightly lit corridor.

I recognized the familiar smells of a hospital, then heard voices, calm and soothing, and felt hands gently moving over me. "Take her to X-ray," one of the voices said.

This must be SF General; I'd been a patient here several years earlier when I'd been shot in the head by an intruder at our then-headquarters on Pier 24½. I'd remained in a locked-in state for almost three weeks—unable to move or speak, but fully cognizant of my surroundings. The staff had been caring and efficient, but I'd never had any desire to come back. Now they wheeled me to X-ray, then took me to a different floor and into a room. It was quiet there, but I could feel and hear the hum of the huge physical plant around me.

After a while a young man in a doctor's coat came in and introduced himself as Dr. Thomas Taylor. "You're fortunate, Ms. McCone," he said. "No broken bones, just nasty scrapes and bruises. You do have a slight concussion, and I'd like to keep you here overnight as a precautionary measure."

"No, I'll recover better at home."

He frowned, looking like a thwarted child. He was young enough to be my son.

"It isn't advisable—" he began.

"You yourself said my injuries aren't serious."

"Protocol dictates—"

"Forget protocol. I'm going home *now*."

"But there may be complications, such as…"

"Such as?"

"…Well, loss of orientation could lead to—"

"I'm not disoriented now, and I don't think the scrapes and bruises and the 'slight concussion' you describe will put me into a coma."

He quit trying to convince me and said instead, "I suggest you discuss this with your husband."

"My—he's here?"

"Yes. I'll get him for you." Dr. Taylor seemed eager to leave the room.

After a minute or so Hy entered, his eyes showing his concern. "You get into the damnedest messes, McCone."

"Not my fault this time."

"You don't seem badly hurt."

"I'm not. Just shaken up and sore. What happened to Denver?"

"Situation defused by someone on the scene."

"How did you know I was here?"

"The hospital called after they found my name on the 'call in case of emergency' card in your purse."

My purse? Oh, right—I'd had it slung across my shoulders under my rain slicker.

He added, "What did you do to Dr. Taylor? He seemed… somewhat intimidated."

"Why? I disagreed with him. I don't want to spend the night here. I'm sure people disagree with that all the time."

"Maybe. But not as…forcibly as you."

"Oh, Ripinsky, come on! The guy looks like he's twelve years old, so I spoke to him as a parent would. Anyway, that's not important. We need to talk about what happened. It was no accident."

"Why do you say that?"

"The driver of the car deliberately tried to run me down."

"You're sure of that?"

"Positive. And I was wearing red—very visible. I swear it has something to do with these private-street vandalisms. That's the reason I was in the Rusty's Meadow neighborhood."

"Can you describe the car?"

"Black. Dirty—there were rain splatters in the dust. The bumper—I think there was an emblem above it. Not a common one like the Mercedes star, but more complicated."

"Did you get a look at the license plate?"

I closed my eyes, trying to remember. "Not a clear look.

But I have a sense that it was one of those black-and-gold commemorative ones they've been issuing for the last few years."

"That's a possible lead. Anything else?"

"No. It all happened pretty fast."

"Would you recognize the car if you saw it again?"

"Yes, I think so."

"I'll have a couple of agency ops canvass the area."

"Good. Now get me out of here!"

"The doc seems to think it's a good idea if you stay, and I agree with him." Before I could speak, he added, "Just take it easy, McCone. You need to rest. I'll be back to pick you up midmorning."

"Deserter!"

He winked at me and left. I took out my frustration by punching my pillow. Then I muttered grumpily for a while. Finally I picked up the TV control and decided to see what was on HBO.

THURSDAY, NOVEMBER 3

When we got to our house, Hy wanted me to spend the rest of the day in bed. I protested, and we settled on my relaxing on the chaise longue in our bedroom. When he left for the office, promising to bring back Chinese takeout, I put on my purple velour robe. After calling the agency to see if there were any new developments—there weren't—I lay back down on the Zebra.

The faux-zebra-skin chaise longue was a joke gift from my brother John that he'd unearthed from the storeroom of a derelict SRO that was being razed in his South of Market neighborhood. It had proved surprisingly comfortable, so we'd installed it in our bedroom. An outstanding fashion statement, we'd decided, to go along with the room's other objets d'arte, including a tank of varicolored rubber jellyfish undulating in blue water, a large gramophone with a polished horn holding silk flowers, and a fake bald eagle flying from one of the rafters.

The two-story house, Spanish revival with cream walls that simulated adobe and a red-tiled roof, stood on a deep corner lot and had redwood decking in the backyard. We'd been lucky to find it just before the prices of San Francisco homes spiraled into the many millions a few years back. I loved its spacious rooms, fireplaces, and updated kitchen, but it wasn't where I wanted to be at the moment. Still, I dozed for a while under a fake-fur throw before the phone rang.

Edmund Spenser, calling to see how I was. He sounded genuinely concerned and a trifle guilty, as if it were somehow his fault that I'd been in the wrong place at the wrong time, and asked if the car that had almost hit me had been identified. I said not yet but assured him that all was well, and when we ended the call, I checked again with the agency. So far none of the ops assigned to my "accident" had been able to find out anything about the car or driver in their canvass of the neighborhood. I thought for a bit, then picked up my laptop, which Hy had left on the bed.

Automobile logos: new, most popular, most expensive, vintage, famous, with wings, design process, designing one's own, with birds, ugliest, with flags, with toads...

This was getting ridiculous. I clicked to go to the next groups: by country, by designer, with fish, with mountains, with wildlife...Even more ridiculous. Determined, I scrolled down.

Silver, gold, matching hood ornaments, foreign, European, Japanese, chrome plated, antique, mounted above grille, suitable for wall hanging...

And then, at the bottom of the page, with the twisted logic that only the internet applies, came a final notation: "comprehensive list with images."

Finally! I clicked the link. What I was looking for came up quickly: Cadillac.

I snatched up my phone to call Derek at the agency. He wasn't in, so I asked for Mick. When I explained the situation to him, he said, "Well, at least you got attacked by a classy car." Then I heard his computer keys tapping. "Cadillac. You got a model?"

"No. Just black with those black-and-orange commemorative plates."

"Narrows it down some. Plate number?"

"Didn't get it."

"What, are your observational skills going downhill?"

"No—I was trying to save *myself* from going downhill."

"Okay, let me work with this for a while and I'll get back to you."

I set down the phone and contemplated the neon jellyfish dancing in their blue water. The bald eagle was swinging on his perch in a draft from one of the windows. Did other people have such objects in their bedrooms? I wasn't sure, but then Hy and I had never been Other People.

The clock downstairs chimed noon. I closed my eyes and slid back down under the furry throw. Later I'd...

3:30 p.m.

The phone rang. Hy.

I grabbed the receiver, dropped it, and fumbled it out from under the bed.

"How you doing?" he asked.

"Okay. You?"

"I'm about to leave for Kansas City. We've got a situation brewing there."

Damn! "Hostage situation?"

"Yeah."

"What kind this time?"

"Another kid with a gun. They seem to be multiplying by the thousands. I'll tell you about it when I get home. Everything okay there?"

"Fine. Let me hear as soon as you can."

It was the usual thing we did when he went into a hostage situation: I didn't wish him luck or tell him to be careful; he didn't display uncertainty or edginess. Hy was an expert negotiator, but such situations can—and do—go bad. So we put a normal face on it. Call the way we interact denial, call it optimism. It doesn't matter—it's the only way the two of us can get through.

FRIDAY, NOVEMBER 4

10:50 a.m.

Hy had called shortly after midnight from Kansas City. He'd talked the kid with the gun into surrendering without anyone being shot, and now he was waiting to hitch a ride with an old buddy who was ferrying a load of electronic equipment in a C-130 from KC to Oakland, with stops in between.

The stops wouldn't put him into Oakland till late today. He could have taken a commercial flight, I thought grumpily, but his innate thriftiness prompted him to take advantage of the offers of the network of friends who piloted for various concerns across the globe. Years earlier his side of our firm had owned a small jet that he'd enjoyed flying, but he'd decided maintaining it was an unnecessary expense. Now the time he spent spelling his old buddies at the controls satisfied his high-flying urges.

I didn't want to waste the day, but I still hurt enough that I huddled in bed as late as was decent and then made a call to one of the most imaginative people I know.

I'd hired Rae Kelleher as my assistant at All Souls Legal Cooperative when I'd finally been promoted upstairs from the closet and my workload had demonstrated a need for help. Rae didn't mind the closet, and she later moved into the big Victorian's attic, where she created a cozy nest in which to hide from her perpetual-student husband. We'd become close friends and—one perpetual-student divorce later—almost relatives when she'd married my former brother-in-law, country music star Ricky Savage.

A lot had changed since that wedding: Ricky's six kids from his marriage to my sister Charlene were mostly on their own or living in London with their mother and her new husband, but they did return periodically and exercise their privilege of moving in and out of the big house in Sea Cliff. Ricky, a record producer as well as a performer, commuted frequently to his company's headquarters in LA. And Rae had become a writer of excellent, popular, and very imaginative suspense novels.

She'd also continued to assist me on some of my cases, one involving a rescue from the icy cold waters of the Bay, another more recently centering on undercover work in an isolated northern California wilderness. No wonder I wanted to consult her on my latest conundrum.

"Sure," she said. "Come on over."

I considered. I felt okay, only a little stiff, and Sea Cliff, an exclusive enclave south of the Gate, wasn't far. Besides, I needed to get out of the house. "Okay, give me an hour or so."

"Great! But watch out for Wesley."

"Who's Wesley?"

"The new cat."

"What happened to Jack?"

"He's still here, but he knows to keep from getting underfoot. Wesley hasn't learned that yet."

I shook my head. It seemed to me they'd once also had a dog, but I couldn't place what had happened to him.

"Anyway," Rae added, "I'm free all day today, and I'll make us big sandwiches."

"You're on."

12:55 p.m.

Fog was rolling in from the Gate as I pulled into the driveway of Rae and Ricky's big redwood-and-glass house on the bluff above China Beach. The vista—Golden Gate Bridge to the north, Marin Headlands straight across, and to the southwest endless ocean—was obscured, and rain started as I scurried down the driveway and let myself in by the kitchen door.

Rae was at the central island, making the promised sandwiches. Her red-gold curls were riotous in the damp air, and she was bundled in a long green snuggly garment. Through the glass doors I could see a roaring fire in the central pit in the living room.

"Hey," she said. "Take off your coat. You want a Snuggie? I've got extras on the rack."

I doffed the coat, selected one of the voluminous garments—blue—and pulled it over my head.

"Where's Mrs. Wellcome?" I asked. Mrs. W was their aptly named housekeeper; more of a family member than an employee, she'd helped them raise the three younger kids, whom the family had called "the Little Savages." Mrs. W preferred to call them "the hellions."

"Mrs. W is off on one of her mysterious excursions, this one involving a garment bag containing a formal dress and a silver-haired gentleman with a chauffeured limo."

"She does get around, doesn't she?"

"More than most of us." Rae paused, gave me a searching look. "What's wrong?"

"Oh, the usual with Hy—a 'situation' in Kansas City. And now he's hitching a ride home with a buddy. God knows where that'll take him."

"But he always comes back, doesn't he?"

"So far, yes. I don't want to talk about it."

"Then we won't. There's white wine chilled in the fridge, and red open in the living room. I suggest we sit by the fire; I sure don't want to look out at the gloom."

"Me either. And I'll take red." I went to one of the loungers that swiveled to afford a view of either the gloom or the firepit, turned it around, and propped my feet up. Rae appeared carrying two wineglasses and a plate of sandwiches.

"So where's himself today?" I asked, meaning Ricky.

"LA, working on the schedule for the band's springtime tour. He'll be back soon. Listen to me: springtime tour, and it isn't even Thanksgiving."

"Time goes fast." I sipped some of the wine she'd poured me, a very good zinfandel. "So are you ready for my latest case rundown?"

"Sure." As I went over the details, she drank, ate, and jotted down notes on a legal pad. When I finished, she sat, tapping her pencil on her upper teeth for a moment, then went to the kitchen and came back with a long piece of butcher's paper that she spread on the hardwood floor.

"Schematics," she said. "Get your butt over here."

By the time I sat down beside her, she'd drawn a large rectangle with various shapes protruding from it.

"This," she said, "is San Francisco."

"I'd've known it anywhere."

"Wait till I dress it up on my computer—then you won't be laughing. Now, we have—so far—four and maybe five private streets." She began making circles with her felt-tip. "Rowan Court. Bancroft Lane. Maynard Way. Rusty's Meadow. And possibly Herrera Terrace. All in different parts of the city. All in different socioeconomic areas. You said none of the residents know each other?"

"Not before this Coalition for the Preservation of Private Streets was formed."

"And there's some doubt as to who formed it?"

"I've got Hank looking into that. As well as who the rightful owners of the land are."

"Well, that's necessary information if we're going to proceed. So was there anyone on the coalition who *didn't* want to hire you?"

"I don't know. No one mentioned it if so."

"Find out." Rae got up, went back to the recliners, and sat in one, putting up its footrest.

I followed her. "Hy and I have speculated on some possible explanations. First, the outrageous cost of real estate in the city. When the last few homes in decent neighborhoods started to sell for more than a million dollars a few years ago, I knew there'd be no stopping it."

"Well, average single-family homes throughout the state have now arrived at the one-point-five-million mark. Equivalent homes here in the city are even more outrageous. I've seen recent listings as high as four-point-seven and seven-point-five million. And just last week—one for forty-five million."

"My God! What can you possibly get for forty-five million?"

"History. Location. And I suspect a lot of costly renovation work."

"How come you're so knowledgeable about real estate prices? You and Ricky aren't thinking of moving, are you?"

"Hell, no! Not with all this stuff we've collected, not to mention the crap the kids have left behind. No, the thing is, Ricky and I have started this little foundation."

"Tell me about it."

"Well, we were going on a few months ago about how hard it is for families who need to be here for their jobs to find housing. People who want to own have to go way out in the San Joaquin Valley, and then they have to get up at three or four in the morning to drive in or take the bus. One thing led to another, and he said, 'Why don't we do something about it?'"

"And?"

"We went to our legal eagle—"

"That would be Hank."

"Of course! Do you think we'd entrust something like this to anybody else? And we set it up that we will buy distressed properties and rent them at below the going rate to qualified individuals."

"And who will these qualified individuals be?"

"Poor or homeless people who are motivated to build up a little sweat equity in a future home."

"Sounds good."

"In theory, yes. Hank warned us that there may be repercussions—stuff along the lines of 'Rich Couple Take Advantage of Homeless' or 'Superstar's Foundation a Publicity Ploy.'"

"Well, screw 'em if they're that small-minded."

"Exactly what Ricky said."

"I said what?"

He came into the room as quietly as he'd entered the house, shedding his water-splotched raincoat and draping it over a chair. Droplets stood out on his dark-brown hair. Ricky had always been handsome, but he was one of those men who grow more attractive with age, and age had also given him a certain presence that transcended even what he conveyed on the stage.

Rae went to hug him, and over her head he said to me, "Hi, Trouble."

He'd taken to calling me that a few years ago when it had occurred to him that whenever I ended up in serious trouble, I also ended up in one of their guest rooms. I must have looked pretty down, because he perched on the edge of my chair and put his arm around my shoulders. "Cheer up," he said. "It can't be all that bad."

It was that attitude, I thought, that had taken him through all the lean years. A true son of Bakersfield, California's capital of country-and-western music, he'd left school at sixteen to form his own band; it had played for years up and down the state, mostly performing Ricky's tunes, but it wasn't until a record producer had heard a demo of his catchy "Cobwebs in the Attic of My Mind" that the band had caught on. In the meantime, he'd spotted my younger sister Charlene from the bandstand at a high school dance in San Diego, married her, and had the first of the Little Savages.

After "Cobwebs" became a major hit, the lean years passed. He and Charlene moved upward—better houses, better schools for the kids, better everything. But Ricky hadn't been able to resist the lure of celebrity; he'd had countless affairs, and Charlene had been driven into the arms of Vic Christiansen, a guest lecturer in international finance at USC, where she'd been pursuing a degree. The marriage crumbled, and Ricky credited Rae with helping him pick up the pieces and move on. Their marriage was solid; Ricky was a reformed man. And Charlene, now living in London, where Vic, with her assistance, managed a major international money fund, couldn't have been happier.

I was about to ask Ricky how the spring tour was shaping up when a black-and-white blur streaked across the room and began biting his ankles. Wesley, the new cat.

Ricky detached him and held him up at eye level. The two stared solemnly at each other, then both blinked, and Ricky set Wesley on the floor.

"Savage—the tamer of savage beasts," I said.

Ricky watched Wesley as he sped off to the kitchen. "I think the beast's tamed *me*. So what's going on?"

I gave him a brief outline of the current case.

He got up, went to the bar cart, and opened some more wine. Refilled Rae's and my glasses, then poured himself some bourbon.

"We've been going over possible motives," I told him.

"Real estate came to mind," Rae said, returning from the kitchen with salsa and chips. Wesley followed hopefully.

Ricky asked, "You tell Shar about our foundation?"

"Yes, but I didn't get around to asking her if she and Hy would contribute." She turned to me. "Will you?"

"Of course."

"Money or time?"

"Both."

"Thanks. Now, one thing that came to my mind is that these attacks are a smoke screen. Something, you know, to draw attention away from what's really going on."

"Like what?" I asked.

"I haven't gotten that far. I'm still looking into the real estate situation in town; most of the important properties are in the hands of the big corporations, like the Carlyle Group, Starr Holdings, and Shorenstein Services. There's also a couple of companies that advertise owning your own home on a time-share basis—five or six people going in on a luxury property and splitting up the use of it, with a company to do the management. Since time-shares have gotten bad press, they try to describe it as a new concept, but it's really the same old thing."

"And you don't think that's the aim here? To acquire the properties and then market them?"

"It doesn't feel right somehow."

"What about this being the doing of an enemy of some of the residents?" Ricky asked.

"Hard to believe that someone has enemies among that many groups of people in such diverse areas."

I frowned. "I agree. But it's also hard to believe the attacks are purely random."

"No, not random. There has to be some motivation behind them."

We were silent for a while. A strong gust of wind from the northwest smacked against the seaside windows. I turned my head, saw a stormy gray sky refracted through huge droplets. It was still raining, but mistily now.

"Diffuse," Rae said. "The motive, I mean. That could be part of it."

I looked at her, then back at where she was staring at the rain-splattered windows. I understood what she meant.

"Yes, diffuse," I said. "Like a circle in the water caused by something falling into it. The circle expands, reaches out on all sides, encountering—and affecting—everything in its path. Whether the things are related or not is irrelevant."

The doorbell rang. Hank announced himself through the speaker, and Rae went to let him in. He asked as he shed his coat, "Anybody here come up with any revelations yet?"

"We're talking about a ripple effect," I said.

"Wasn't that what we called it after we drank too much bad wine in college?"

Everybody groaned.

"A ripple effect," he said, sitting down on the hearth and grabbing a handful of chips, "is a phenomenon such as this cat getting booted across the room for biting my ankles."

Wesley looked up at him, then trotted over and sat docilely on Rae's foot.

"Sometimes I think that cat understands English," Ricky muttered.

"Okay," I said. "Any ideas what caused this so-called ripple effect?"

"The one thing that comes to mind," Hank said, "is the land grab when that couple tried to buy up the common area of Presidio Terrace for back taxes and then resell it to the residents for megabucks."

"That was a number of years ago, and the courts ruled in favor of the residents."

"Yes, but maybe somebody dug up the old story and

used it as a basis for causing trouble to further their own scheme."

I shrugged. "Maybe."

Hank said, "Well, I did gather some information about this guy who claims he started the coalition—Sam Sage."

"False claim?"

"Yes. He's a member of the coalition, nothing more. But he's evidently running a scam to get donations over the internet. I plan to pay him a visit tomorrow and make a few succinct comments on fraud."

"I'd love to be there to hear them—"

My cell rang, interrupting the conversation. Hy.

"Where are you?" I asked.

"Still waiting for my buddy in Kansas City. Anything new to report there?"

"Not so far. I'm at Rae and Ricky's, brainstorming with them and Hank."

"Well, that's a combination that's sure to produce results." He sounded distracted. "Listen, I'll let you know as soon as I'm on my way to Oakland."

The phone connection was broken, but the emotional one stretched strong between us.

SATURDAY, NOVEMBER 5

2:41 a.m.

Ringing sounds woke me from a sound sleep. My damn phone. Groggily, I squinted at the clock, then fumbled for the cell on the nightstand and growled a hello.

"McCone?" The voice was familiar, but distorted by anxiety.

"Who's this?"

"...need help."

Then it connected. "Sam Sage! Why're you calling at this ungodly hour—"

"They're after me!"

"What?"

"Gotta get away from here!"

"Where are you?"

"My place. Get here fast. Or else I gotta take the money and run."

The line went dead. I was out of bed and pulling on clothes immediately.

Sam hadn't been putting on one of his jokes; he'd been truly frightened.

3:17 a.m.

The rain had stopped, but thick, dark clouds roiled across the sky. Mud oozed down Bancroft Lane, so I left my car at the corner and slogged through it, glad I'd thought to wear my waterproof hiking shoes. It was strangely silent up there above the muted lights of the city. The only sounds were those of trees shedding water and the persistent wind.

I was halfway up the trail, opposite the urban dumping ground, when the ground got slicker; to keep my balance, I practically had to crawl around a slight curve to Sam's building. The battered white truck that had been parked in front during my last visit was gone.

I rounded the corner to the other side of the building. The iron-barred door stood partway open. I seized the mallet attached to the bell and whacked it; the sound echoed hollowly within. Empty silence followed. Frowning, I pushed the door open a little wider, whacked the bell again. Total darkness inside, no lights anywhere. I called for Sam. No response.

What the hell? Had he called me out here and then left? I took out my phone, pressed his number. No ringtone; his device was shut down.

Maybe I'd overreacted. Could Sam's call for help have been a stupid joke? No, he'd sounded genuinely upset and afraid. Normally I wouldn't have put anything past the little bastard, but this didn't feel like a prank. Something must've happened to make him run.

I reached around the door frame and felt for a light switch, found an old-fashioned plate with buttons. It didn't work. There must be another source of power; that satellite dish couldn't operate off such primitive equipment. I took my flashlight from my bag and shone it around. What I could see of the front room looked the same as it had before: oversize yoga mat, assorted lumpy sofas and chairs. I called out again, and when there was still no answer, I stepped inside. The floor coverings were soggy from in-blown rain; a chill wind blasted through, bringing with it the smell of mildew. I moved forward, directing the flashlight's beam ahead and then upward at another brick wall with two archways opening off it; between them, a big banner depicting an evil-eyed bird of prey flapped damply.

Once more I called out. No response. I tried Sam's phone again. Nothing.

I followed the light beam to one of the archways. Bathroom. A tub with a sleeping bag and pillows spread on the floor next to it. A randomly squeezed tube of toothpaste and a brush sat on a glass shelf above an old pedestal sink. A couple of used hand towels hung from a hook. That was all.

I checked the adjacent room: it apparently was used for clothing and storage. A couple of racks positioned at odd angles held jeans and sweats and shirts. I poked through stacks of flattened cardboard cartons and others containing junk. There was a kitchen setup in a far corner, with a counter, motel-size refrigerator, hot plate, and toaster oven. Plates and glasses and cooking equipment sat on a low shelf.

I checked the contents of the small fridge. Nothing but moldy-looking cheese, orange juice a week beyond its use-by date, and a lone desiccated lime.

Where was the evidence of any committee work being done on the premises, as Sam had claimed? Why the large satellite dish on the roof in the absence of computers, TVs, or other electronic devices?

But then the light beam illuminated a portion of the far end of the room that had been partitioned off with heavy plywood. A rough-cut door was centered in it, hinged and secured by hasps and two padlocks. I went over and kicked at it, but it wouldn't move. Threw the weight of my body against it, and only succeeded in hurting my shoulder.

I debated the wisdom of what I was doing. Breaking and entering? Technically, no. Sam had asked me here. The outer door had been open. I had reason to be concerned for his safety. An ordinary citizen would have notified the police and waited, but my professional instincts argued against it; the response time in San Francisco was unconscionably slow, and the fear in Sam's voice had indicated high degree of urgency.

I looked around more carefully. A heavy hammer leaned in a corner. I took it up and swung it, first at the hasp, and then at the hinges. The vibrations from the blows sent painful reverberations up my arms and across my neck and shoulders. I rested, leaning on a nearby sawhorse, then swung again. A crack appeared beside the hasp. Taking a wider stance, I put all my strength into another swing, and the wood splintered. A few more whacks, and I pulled a large portion of the door free.

Inside was an office setup: computer, workstation, printer. All were reasonably new and well maintained. I set my flash beside the keyboard, dragged over a nearby desk chair, and sat; when I hit the Return key, the machine booted up immediately, and a desktop image appeared: "Sageland" in dark-green script against a background of lighter-green leaves and orange California poppies. A dozen desktop files appeared along the right-hand margin, each requiring a password.

A problem for me, but not for Derek Frye, one of the best password busters in the business. I quickly sent the files to his office at the agency and appended an explanation. Then I searched through the machine's other files but found nothing of interest.

A damp wind swirled through the open door, bringing with it an odd feeling of sadness. Sam's life here had been a lonely one, which was probably the reason he'd railed at me about the richness of my own: "Got yourself a big agency now, a building downtown, a house in the Marina, an airplane, even a husband. Doin' good, McCone."

And then, as if he were there beside me, I imagined his caustic voice saying, "Don't you go feeling sorry for me, Superdick."

I wouldn't. I'd made my life, and he'd made his.

The wind was whipping up beyond the outer door. It snapped dried branches from the oaks and pines, brought with it the scent of eucalypti, made the metal roof shudder. Outside, the lights of the city spread out around me, jittering among the tossing vegetation. As I passed down the path beside Sam's building, I stumbled and went down on one knee, steadied myself at the corner. Shapes were moving in the darkness. I heard crackling sounds. A rumbling—

And the night suddenly exploded.

The blast was enormous. It came from nearby, causing the ground to tremble and throwing me on my back on the slope. Flames shot up into the dark sky and burning embers rained down. Noxious fumes enveloped me. Gagging, I pressed my face into the crook of my arm. A windblown ember landed on my wrist, and I quickly brushed it off. Then I lay still, breathing through my mouth.

Everything was very quiet except for the roar of flames. Then people in the neighborhood came outside, shouting, calling out in frightened voices.

"What was that?"

"The goddamn hill's on fire!"

"Are you okay?"

"Watch out! That tree—it's gonna fall!"

"Help!"

I struggled to sit up. Sirens had begun to wail below.

I pushed to my knees, then crawled around the corner. From there I could see what it was that had exploded—the uppermost of the small buildings halfway down the trail. Chunks of brick and smoldering pieces of wood and shingles littered the ground.

It wasn't long before fire trucks came rushing up Bancroft Lane. Personnel jumped down from them, rolled out hoses, went rapidly to work with fire-retardant foam. I knelt beside Sam's building, watching as the flames were extinguished.

"Ma'am? Are you all right?" One of the firemen had spotted me. An anxious soot-smeared face looked out at me from under an SFFD helmet.

"I'm okay. Do you know what caused the explosion?"

"Not yet. But I can make a pretty good guess."

So could I, now. There was a smell in the air like that of rotten eggs. The kind of stench you get when a meth lab blows up.

6:40 a.m.

I'd waited at the scene, given preliminary statements to both fire department and police investigators. No human remains had been found. Neither had Sam Sage, and an APB had been put out on him and his vehicle. The only message on my phone was a text from Hy, finally on his flight back. Reassured, I switched the device off and started home.

On my way, I thought about Sam. Why had he called me? He'd said "they" were after him. Who? Had the persons arrived? Had he eluded them? What did he mean by "Or else I gotta take the money and run?" What money? Proceeds from his meth lab? Run to where?

The explosion: Was Sam responsible for it, or had it been a coincidence, possibly spontaneous? It wouldn't surprise me if he'd been cooking small amounts of meth up there. It was a relatively secluded parcel of land where there weren't any near neighbors to smell any suspicious odors or notice excessive trash dumping. In any case he must have known about it since the little building was downhill from his. Who had rigged the explosion? Maybe some enemy he'd made because of his online vitriol was responsible for the explosion, hoping to take him out?

At home I took a shower to rinse off the dirt and soot, then put in a call to my old friend Deputy Fire Commissioner Lance Grayson at his home in Hayes Valley. Lance and I went way back to the old house on Durant Avenue in Berkeley, where he and his long string of girlfriends had inhabited the room across the hall from mine. A varsity basketball player, he still looked the part, although the last time I'd seen him, I'd noticed that time had receded his curly hair and grayed what was left of it. In his matter-of-fact way, he didn't seem surprised to hear from me so early in the morning.

Yes, he was aware of the incident on Bancroft Way, he said in answer to my question. What was my interest in it?

I explained about my case and Sam Sage's disappearance. "Do your people have anything yet on his whereabouts?"

"Not as far as I know."

"Anything on the cause of the explosion? Accidental or deliberate?"

"Nothing definite yet. But if it was a meth lab, in many cases when those blow up, it's a case of spontaneous combustion. Gases build up within, and even when no one's working there, kaboom. We're working on the accidental theory, but we'll have more details after all the hot spots are out. Tell me, what do you know about Sage?"

"He's an internet scammer, my sources tell me, but I don't have much more information yet."

"When you went to see Sage earlier, did you notice if he had a vehicle?"

"A white Toyota truck. In shabby condition. I didn't notice the plates or model number. But it wasn't there when I went back tonight."

"We'll add that information to the APB."

"Speaking of APBs," I said, "there's something else you should know, Lance." I told him about the Cadillac that had nearly run me down. "I wasn't anywhere near Bancroft Lane, but the property I was visiting was another private street."

"Uh-huh. I'll get that over to our command center and the PD as well. I take it nobody at your agency has picked up anything about the Cadillac or its driver?"

"Not that I've heard."

After we ended our call, I looked at the clock. By now Hy should be landing at Oakland.

Time to check in with the agency. Somebody was always there, no matter what the hour. Derek answered.

"Hey," he said, "I've got some information: A Cadillac of the description of the one that tried to hit you was located on a residential street in Walnut Creek last night. A DMV check named the owner as a Wilson Reed on Noriega Street in the Inner Sunset. I contacted Reed. He said the car disappeared sometime on Thursday night or early Friday morning. He notified the police, and they got back to him last night, returned the car early this morning."

"Was it damaged in any way?"

"No, Reed said it was in great condition. In fact, it looked as if it'd been put through a car wash."

A common ploy when someone's used a vehicle for a crime, making the vehicle's use almost impossible to verify.

"By the way," Derek added, "I'm about to start busting those passwords on the files you sent me earlier. You planning on coming in today?"

"This afternoon, for a while."

"Good. We'll go over what I come up with then."

Okay, I thought as I ended the call, I'd need to talk with the Cadillac's owner, but it was too early to be paying him a visit. I curled up on the living room couch with the cats to pass the time, and it wasn't long before I fell asleep.

9:44 a.m.

I woke with a start, hearing a voice in the kitchen.

"What, did she forget to feed you?" Hy asked.

Alex, the more vocal of the two cats, yowled.

"Well, we'll see about that. Here, tide yourself over with some of these treats."

I went out there, trailing the blanket I'd been wrapped in. Hy was making coffee.

"Quick trip," I said, hugging him.

"Not as quick as I'd hoped, since we got hung up on one of our stops, which is why I'm later than planned. How come you were sleeping on the couch?"

I explained about the events at Sam Sage's property as we drank our coffee.

"Jesus," Hy said, "that's damned scary. You could've been killed or at least badly injured."

"Now that I think about it, I realize it was stupid to go out there without backup. But he sounded so afraid, and I didn't want to waste time."

"Riding to the rescue, huh?"

"You know me."

"That I do, and I love you for it. But please try to be more careful in the future. I don't want to lose you."

"I will—I promise. Anyway, I've got a lead on the Cadillac that almost ran me down. I'm going to have to go out to the Inner Sunset and talk with its owner. It shouldn't take long."

"Want to meet me at the agency? I've got work to catch up on there."

"See you in a couple of hours."

11:21 a.m.

The house on Noriega Street where the Cadillac's owner, Wilson Reed, lived was a three-story cube of whitewashed brick with stains from its gutters streaking the façade. The garage door was raised, and sounds of hammering came from within. I parked across the drive, went up, and knocked on the door frame.

A tall, thin man was nailing a piece of plywood to a pair of sawhorses. When he heard me, he set down his hammer and came toward me, wiping perspiration from his bald head. I introduced myself and handed him my card.

"Oh yeah, about the Caddy," he said. "Cops said somebody might be coming around. Damnedest thing. It's in great shape."

"You have any idea who might have stolen it?"

He shrugged. "Local kids joyriding, maybe."

"So you didn't see it taken."

"No, I was in bed asleep. It was gone in the morning when I got up."

"I assume it was locked. How do you suppose the thief got into it?"

"Not by jimmying the door. No damage at all, not even a scratch. And I sure didn't leave a key inside."

Thieves had all sorts of ingenious ways of stealing cars; that was why there were so many incidents these days. It didn't really matter how my would-be murderer had managed it. I said, "I'd like to get a look at the car, if you don't mind."

"Be my guest." He motioned to it and went back to his carpentry project.

The car was clean and free of scratches or dents. Nothing inside; it was as clean as if it had just been driven off the showroom floor. I returned to the garage, and Wilson and I chatted briefly about the frequency of auto-related crime in the city before I left.

12:17 p.m.

When I got to the M&R building, I went to the research department and found Derek at his computer, immersed in a file.

He waved me in and said, "This Jill Madison. Her background's kind of interesting. She's from Seattle, came here for the better weather." He chuckled. While our weather beats Seattle's, it's not exactly a draw for someone who doesn't appreciate dampness.

He went on. "She's something of a prodigy—before Seattle she went to Yale, had a Rhodes Scholarship to Oxford her junior year. Has a small trust fund from a wealthy aunt that she spends carefully, so she doesn't have to work—or works minimally, like at this candy place in the Mission. Devotes a lot of her time to those online sites that attempt to solve cold cases, particularly ones that deal with missing persons. Has actually solved a couple of disappearances."

That interested me; I'd solved a couple of cold cases in my day too. "Oh? Which ones?"

"Remember Rod Keenan? The Silicon Valley engineer who disappeared three years ago? Madison found him living quietly with a second family in Idaho. And Kelley Clarkson? She turned up running a dude ranch in Wyoming."

"Either of them want to return to their former lives?"

"Nope. I guess if you go to great lengths to disappear, you really don't want to be found."

That had been my experience. Still, I'd like to talk to Jill about her reasons for frequenting those sites. "Anything on the Koslowskis? The family that once owned Rusty's Meadow up on the hill?"

"A title search showed no survivors. I also talked with the other residents of the Meadow. None of them were home the day you almost got run over. The woman on the gate was coming back from a bathroom break when she saw you falling and didn't notice the car."

"Good work, Derek."

"Thanks. Anything else?"

"Not for now. But you know me..."

"Right. You'll be in touch."

1:14 p.m.

In my office I checked for coffee, found the carafe empty. Too late to make a fresh batch, I reasoned, but still, it made me grumpy. I was frowning when I went in to see Hy in his office.

He looked up at me and asked, "You okay?"

"Yes and no." I outlined what I'd found out about Jill Madison. "And I'm still grappling with the question of Sam Sage."

He got up, motioned for me to join him on his couch. "So what's the deal with this Sage person? Did he die in the explosion?"

I settled in against his shoulder, curling my legs next to me. "No sign of him."

"Not even bits and pieces?"

"No. The fire department is leaning toward the theory that the explosion was an accident. I'm not so sure."

"Why do you suppose Sage called you?"

"Good question. He sounded scared on the phone. Maybe somebody he was involved with was threatening him."

"Who could that be?"

"I have no idea."

"And why turn to you for help?"

"Another good question. The man doesn't particularly like or trust me."

"That meth lab—where was it?—oh, right, in a shed. If he blew it up of his own volition—why? It exposed him as a criminal."

"So maybe it was an accident. Maybe somebody kidnapped him independent of that."

"And you saw nobody while you were up there?"

"Not a soul, although the wind was pretty wild. It might've covered up a lot of sounds."

"So what tack do we take from here?"

"*We?*"

"We're in this together. McCone & Ripinsky, remember?"

"But don't you have—?"

"Anything else on my plate? No, not at the moment."

"Well, welcome aboard, pardner." I shook his hand. "Let's go find out what's happened to Sam Sage."

1:53 p.m.

The research floor at M&R is usually quiet, although there's always plenty going on there. The tapping of computer keys, whirring of printers, and rustling of papers make for a subdued environment, except for the occasional triumphant yell when one or another of the employees scores a hit on info they're searching for. This afternoon, however, it was as quiet as a tomb.

Derek had been at his desk for more than six hours when

Hy and I arrived and was hungry and eager to get out. He suggested the Recovery Room, where they concoct the best grilled-cheese-and-bacon sandwiches in the world, so we strolled two blocks over to Howard Street.

The Recovery is one of those old working-class bars that still populate corners of the city. It's dark and quiet, with cracked leatherette booths and a worn linoleum floor, and its long plank bar is backed by a mirror and dusty shelves of bottles. The booths and stools are comfortable, due to having been broken down by many assorted rumps, and the pinball machine and jukebox have long ago been decommissioned, providing an oasis of silence.

We took seats in one of the booths and ordered. Derek spread out his printouts of Sam Sage's recovered files.

The files contained an odd jumble of subjects: conspiracy theories, attacks on local and state politicians, critiques of the city planning commission, revisionist history, support for ultraconservative clergy, and negative commentary on entertainers and restaurateurs. Ricky was described as a singer who should go back to Nashville (he was from Bakersfield), and Superdick herself was surprised to see that she was classified as a neo-Nazi.

Sam had missed his calling as a writer of fantasy. Trouble was, nothing very revealing emerged from all this crap, except that the Sage family owned a cottage on Cottonwood Lake in eastern Santa Clara County. The address was 22701 North Shore Drive.

Hy asked, "Could that be where he went?"

Derek studied his notes. "Cottonwood Lake is pretty remote—south of Highway 130, almost to the Stanislaus County line."

I rummaged in my bag for a notebook. "Give me the address again."

Hy said, "You're thinking of going there?"

"Why not?"

"Sure. Why not?"

"You're coming with?"

"Of course. Didn't you say, 'Welcome aboard, pardner?'"

2:45 p.m.

Saturday-afternoon traffic on Bay Area freeways is always a mess on any route we could have chosen to get to eastern Santa Clara County, but the San Francisco Peninsula was particularly clogged today, so we cut over to the East Bay, found getting past San Jose a nightmare, finally slipped out of the bottleneck on Highway 101, and took a small, secondary road toward the hamlet of Analy.

Most people in the Bay Area equate Santa Clara County with its major city of San Jose, Silicon Valley, and Levi's Stadium, home of the 49ers football team. But east of that urban hub, the land stretches arid and barren, mostly treeless and served by few roads. The housing tracts that clog the valley stop abruptly, as if their developers have acknowledged the inhospitality of the terrain.

The town of Analy wasn't much, but it afforded pleasant relief from the smog-ridden stretches of freeway. A grocery, a pharmacy, a bar and grill, a plaza with a fountain that spurted no water—that was it. Finally a roadside sign appeared for the turnoff for Cottonwood Lake: red on blue, badly weathered, advertising "Lodging and Fine Dining."

Hy said, "A relic of the past."

We continued on the bumpy access road, and then the lake spread before us, stagnant and slimed with algae. The sites I'd accessed before we left the city had said most of the recreation areas were closed because of the drought, and that the lake, formerly a thriving reservoir, was down to 3 percent of its usual capacity. It was late in the year for algae bloom, but the extreme heat waves of the fall had upset the plants' usual schedule. The air, even with our car windows closed, stank of dead fish and moldering vegetation. A few old buildings hugged the shore: Crystal Marina Inn, Riviera Yacht Club, the Shores Motel. All were closed up and deserted. A trailer park housed broken-down and vacant mobile homes from the eighties, and the other small homes were shuttered. A sign on a crumbling concrete wall marked the entrance to North Shore Drive, where the Sage house was located.

Mick had sent me the property records for the site. Sam Sage still owned the cottage. A photo on Street View showed a small, square clapboard building with boarded-up windows and a pebbled yard stretching down to the water. There were no records of phone service. The house was even more depressing than the nearby town: cracks in the façade, a leaning stovepipe chimney, broken front steps. There was no sign of Sam's battered white truck.

As we pulled in, Hy said, "If he ran here, he's got to be seriously depressed—and afraid."

I asked, "Are you carrying?"

"No. You?"

"My .38's in my bag."

"You don't seriously think we'll need firepower?"

"We might. Look what happened to the meth lab."

Hy nodded, studying the house. "Well, let's go."

Up close, the house looked as if it might be inhabited: a window was partly open, and a tattered sheer curtain flapped in the wind. I opened my purse for easy access to the .38 before knocking. Inside there was a scuffling of feet, and then a woman's voice shouted, "Okay, okay, I'm coming!"

The woman who opened the door was tall and full breasted, with curly orange hair. Her blue eyes were large and stared fixedly at us, and then she cocked her head in a way that reminded me of a parrot.

"Yeah?" she said.

"We're looking for Sam Sage. Is he at home?"

She looked Hy and me over warily. In our city clothes, we didn't fit in out here. "Are you guys cops?"

"No." There didn't seem to be any need for my gun. I took out one of my business cards before closing my purse and handed it to her.

She squinted at it. "So you want Sammy? Shit. He give you this address?"

"It's his place, isn't it?"

"Yeah, it's his, but he said I'd have exclusive use of it till next spring. Damn that little weasel! He was here, but then he left."

I asked, "When was he here?"

"Last night for a while."

"Did he say where he was going?"

"Nope. And now I'm stuck with his shit. What am I gonna do with his smelly old sleeping bag and dirty laundry? He's here, he's not here. He comes, he goes. Who knows when or why? But I've had it. On my next trip to the dump, the stuff's gone. Next time he comes and tries to move in on me, I'm gone too. Guy's an asshole, why I ever put up with him I don't know."

"Did he tell you about the explosion at his San Francisco property?"

"Yeah, but not much. He said somebody was out to get him and he needed to hole up."

"Did he say who?"

"No."

"Out to get him for what reason?"

"He wouldn't tell me that either. Then this morning he was gone—along with a hundred bucks from my purse."

She seemed not to know about the meth, and I saw no reason to enlighten her. I said, "Would you mind letting us look at the stuff he left here?"

She opened the door and motioned us toward a narrow flight of stairs. "Go ahead. I'm Amber, by the way. Amber Lee. I lost my job in Silicon Valley and couldn't afford my apartment there. When Sam offered this place, it seemed a good solution till something else turned up. It's close enough to San Jose so I could job-hunt. But after the hundred bucks, I've had it with him."

"How did you and Sam meet?"

"Diablo Valley Polytechnic. He was kind of an internet geek. I was going to study coding, but I couldn't hack it, so I just took a lower course and got placed in a job with a packaging company. We didn't see each other, but then we reconnected at a class reunion in, I think, 2020. We've been on and off since then. Come on in, I'll show you his stuff."

The house was one big room with a hallway leading back to a bath and a kitchen. Thrift-shop furnishings, sentimental posters of kittens, a big-screen TV. The sleeping bag was rolled in a corner, a duffel bag beside it. The duffel contained dirty clothing. I sifted through it, then paid closer attention to the bag. It had pouches sewn into it for camping gear: battery-powered can opener, butane lighter, fold-up utensils. A hole in the corner of one pouch opened into the interior of the bag; I felt below it, found a small bulge. Dug out a newspaper-wrapped parcel and opened it.

A diamond ring. Platinum, with old-fashioned filigree and a large brilliant-style stone. I'd seen it—or one very like it—before.

"This yours?" I asked Amber.

She was staring greedily at it, but shook her head. "I've never seen it before."

Where had I seen the ring? I thought. *Where?*

A woman's hands, steepled against her lips, her eyes sheened with fear...

I asked, "Do you know Theresa Segretti? Or her husband, Davis?"

"No. Who're they?"

"Friends of Sam."

"Sam never introduced me to any of his friends. Like he was ashamed of me or something."

Hy said, "All right if we take the ring and the rest of his things with us?"

"Yeah, sure. Like I told you, I don't want nothing more to do with him."

"I'll give you a receipt."

"Don't bother. He's outta my life."

It surprised me that Amber would give up a valuable ring so easily. But maybe she, like me, suspected that it might lead to serious trouble.

6:34 p.m.

Back in the city, Rowan Court was silent in the growing dark. Hy and I parked near the gatehouse and walked up to the Segretti house. At first it seemed no one was home, but then Theo opened the door, and judging from her expression, she wasn't glad to see me.

"If this is coalition business," she said, "you'd better come back tomorrow morning, when I'll be free to tend to it."

I smelled gin on her breath. And she probably had a drug or drugs in her too; her pupils were very dilated.

"We need to talk now." I slipped through the door, Hy right behind me.

Theo didn't protest. She shrugged wearily and ushered us into the overly decorated living room. I introduced Hy, and we took seats on the spindly furniture arranged around the fireplace. I removed the newspaper-wrapped packet from my bag and placed the diamond ring on the glass-topped coffee table. Theo said nothing, staring at it as if mesmerized.

"This is yours," I said.

She nodded.

"Don't you want to know where I got it?"

"From Sam Sage, I suppose."

"He left it and other personal effects in a house he owns near Analy, in Santa Clara County."

"He owns a house?"

"He rents it out to a friend, Amber Lee." I told her the address, asked, "How did he come to have your ring?"

No reply.

"Did you give it to him?"

"I ... Yes."

"Why?"

"He was going to tell."

"Tell what? To whom?"

She shook her head.

"Did what he threatened to tell have anything to do with the vandalisms or the coalition?"

She continued to stare glassily at the ring.

I nodded to Hy. Time for him to join the questioning.

He leaned forward and put his hand on her arm. "Mrs. Segretti, did Sam Sage threaten you? Hurt you in any way?"

No response. Her hands twitched nervously in her lap.

"I mean," he went on, "he has a reputation as someone who enjoys hurting people. Especially women."

As far as I knew, Sam had no such reputation, but Hy was good at spinning a tale that would open up a subject: the low, sympathetic tone was an invitation to confide, based on his own gut feelings for what would work. As he touched Theo Segretti's arm, he seemed like a father confessor.

Segretti's dilated eyes were moist now. She fumbled in her sweater pocket for a handkerchief, and damned if Hy didn't have one ready to supply her with. "He said he'd get me," she whispered.

"Why? For what?"

"... It has to do with ... Davis, my husband. Sam claimed Davis was into something really bad. He was going to go to the police, so I gave him my ring to keep him quiet."

"Why the ring? Why not money?"

"He wanted it as security, since I can't access my money that easily."

"What day was this?"

"I don't remember."

"Think."

Headshake. "I can't."

I asked, "Did you access the funds to give to Sam?"

"No. They're held by a trust; I couldn't access them as quickly as he wanted."

"Have you heard from him since the explosion at his property?"

"No, not a word."

"Tried to contact him?"

She shook her head violently. "Why would I?"

"Do you have any idea where he might be?"

"No."

"Did you know about his meth business?"

"God, no!"

"You said he claimed your husband was involved in something bad. What kind of something?"

"I don't know. Davis and I never discuss business."

"He's an importer, right?"

"Yes. Of Asian arts. He's been out of the country for ten days."

"Where can I reach him?"

"I don't know."

"Are you often unable to reach him when he travels?"

"... Well, Davis and I ... we live very independently."

They were estranged?

"Surely you have a contact number for him? An office number?"

"... No."

"A number for his attorney? Or a business manager?"

"No!"

Hy was fiddling with his smartphone and didn't look up. Theo Segretti took advantage of the silence by getting to her feet. "I want you people out of here," she said. "You've intruded enough."

I said, "But you're one of the principals of the coalition that hired me—"

"Consider your employment terminated as of now."

I was going to argue, but Hy stood and motioned for me to join him. Segretti didn't bother showing us to the door.

Halfway down the court to the car, I said, "Why did you cave in like that?"

"We wouldn't have gotten anywhere with her, not in her condition. I think you'd better try contacting the other members of the coalition. Now. Before she can get to them and tell them she's fired you."

I slid into my car and punched the various numbers on speed dial. Busy signal at the first. Only voice mail at three others, including that of Jane Christhof, the coalition chairman. Saturday-evening silence. I left call-back messages. Hy was leaning on the side of the car, still working with his device. He punched in a number, said, "Mick? Hy. You at home?...Have time to meet with McCone and me?... Good. We'll see you within the hour."

"Why Mick?" I asked when he disconnected.

"We've already loaded Derek up with this case, and Mick is prepared to assist. He might lend us a fresh perspective, in view of what I suspect."

"And that is?"

"From my cursory searches just now, what I suspect is that Davis Segretti doesn't exist."

8:01 p.m.

A couple of years earlier, my nephew Mick had sold his high-rise condo in the South of Market district and bought a small art deco building on Telegraph Hill near Coit Tower, a few blocks from Plum Alley, where Ted and Neal lived. The bottom floor was garage and storage, and the second had two bedrooms and a combined work area and adult playroom. He buzzed us in from up there, and we met among a welter of deep, comfortable furnishings, plush rugs, and a large-screen viewing station. A well-equipped kitchen took up a fair amount of space, and from it I could smell enticing odors—stew, maybe?

Mick greeted me in his usual way—a bear hug that lifted me some two feet off the floor. He ushered us inside, supplied drinks without asking—wine for me, IPAs for Hy and him. While Hy briefed him on the case, I tried Jane Christhof again and finally reached her. She said she'd be at home all evening and told me to stop by anytime before eleven. Hy finished telling Mick about the lack of evidence—tax records, property deeds, various accounts—that made him doubt Davis Segretti's existence. Mick listened without asking questions, making notations on a smartphone, then excused himself and went to the big screen. For fifteen minutes we could hear him muttering to himself occasionally: "Yeah…No…Well, maybe…Significant…"

Finally he went to the kitchen, stirred the stew, and returned to us.

"Segretti is not all that common a name," he said. "Most prominent on the Net is one of the Watergate conspirators from the seventies who's still capitalizing on his dubious fame, but he's got no connection to this inquiry. I just did a wide property search, checked business listings, looked at available tax records, and so forth. Nothing."

"So who owns the house on Rowan Court?" I asked.

"A corporation, WHS, well known for helping clients conceal assets."

"Can you go deeper on WHS?"

He smiled. "Sure. And I will."

I said, "Try linking the Segrettis to Sam Sage, the influencer who disappeared after a meth lab near his Russian Hill property blew up the other night."

"I'm familiar with Sage. He's a nano-influencer."

"Meaning?"

"Has a low following on sites like TikTok, YouTube, and Instagram. A thousand to ten thousand max."

I said, "I can see why. The stuff he puts out there is outrageous and erroneous."

"Doesn't stop people from believing it, though. There's a whole segment of the population who will believe anything if it's published in the media—print, TV, and especially electronic. And this is nothing new: consider the panic after the radio transmission of *The War of the Worlds* back in 1938."

Mick was a fan of old radio shows and had played the performance for me a while ago: H. G. Wells's radio drama had believably depicted a series of alien invasions in New Jersey and caused a serious panic, sending gullible residents in the vicinities of the fictional landing sites scrambling for their lives from their homes and places of business.

I said, "So now we have categories for these so-called influencers?"

"Sure: nano; micro—ten thousand to a hundred thousand; macro—one hundred thousand to one million; and mega—one million or more. Mostly they're aimed at marketing products: 'So-and-so swears by Allure Shampoo'; 'Charlie Celebrity wants you to try Smashing Cherries Lipstick.' But others are political, and some are downright sinister."

"Sinister in what way?"

"Promoting child porn. Claiming events like school shootings never happened. Advocating for all kinds of violence."

"Makes me glad I don't deal much with social media."

"Makes me think that M&R should be monitoring these sites more closely."

"Maybe we should," Hy said. "Can you get us information about what that would entail?"

"Sure can. It might be a good detail to get Patrick and his boys on."

Patrick Neilan was an excellent all-around operative, and now that they were almost grown, the two boys he'd raised as a single father were showing a desire to join the agency.

"Great idea," I said. "Now about Sam Sage: Any indications about where he might have gone to hide out? We've already traced him to a property he owns in Santa Clara County, but the trail ends there."

"I'll work on it. You guys want to stay for dinner? I'm making posole—Mexican pork-and-hominy stew."

"Yes," we both said at once.

"Great. It'll be on the table late, though—nine-thirty, maybe not till ten."

"Perfect," I told him. That would give me time to drop in on Jane Christhof.

9:13 p.m.

Jane Christhof's home was on Larkin Lane—one of the private streets that so far hadn't been vandalized, off California Street near the approach to the Golden Gate Bridge. It had an imposing brick façade covered in ivy and was set a mere six feet off the sidewalk behind a tall black iron fence. Christhof herself was what you would expect of a person who lived in such a dwelling. Well coiffed and made up, she was dressed in what I thought might be a society matron's uniform for a weekend night when she had nothing much going on: pink silk lounging pajamas, multiple strands of pearls draped around her long neck, and stylish rings on the fingers of both hands.

She led me into a casual living room, offered me refreshment, which I declined, and then proceeded to berate me for my lack of progress on the coalition's investigation.

"Before we go into that, Ms. Christhof," I said, "I'd like to ask you why you brought this inquiry to my agency in the first place."

"Well..." She looked unsure, touching her fingertips to the pearls. "Well, everyone knows you're one of the best firms in the city."

"But someone must have suggested us. I can't imagine you make a habit of employing investigators."

She smiled weakly. "No, of course not. Not meaning to denigrate what you do, but in my set, it's not usually necessary to require..."

I raised my eyebrows and smiled sarcastically. "Not necessary to require the services of a firm such as mine until one of your set has a compelling need to do so."

She looked ashamed, dipping her face down.

"So who brought us to your attention?"

"To the coalition's attention, you mean."

I was wearying of this semantic game.

Before I could comment, however, Christhof went on, "Really, Ms. McCone, I believe we made a mistake in naming Theresa Segretti as your main contact. The woman is—"

"Yes?"

"...Not very responsible."

"In what way?"

She shook her head.

"What about her husband, Davis?"

"Oh, he's long out of the picture."

"They're divorced?"

She shrugged.

"Did you know him?"

"Only the idea of him."

"The *idea* of him?"

"He's reclusive. Whenever anyone requests he accompany Theo to one of our set's important functions, he's either too busy or out of the country. There are times when protocol calls for her to have an escort, and she comes up with one, but often they're unsuitable."

"In what way?"

She waved a hand as if I should understand. "Not properly connected. Poorly dressed. You know."

Sounded like some of my best friends.

"Are you aware," I said, "that Theo Segretti fired me this afternoon?"

She put a hand to her throat, genuinely surprised. "I had no idea! Why would she do that?"

"I believe it was because I questioned her too closely about her husband."

"Ridiculous! She can't do that!"

"Does this mean you don't support the termination?"

"Absolutely not. I—and the other members of the coalition—want you to continue as planned."

But minutes before, she'd been criticizing me for my lack of progress. I decided not to push her and stood. "Fine," I said. "I'll report to you soonest."

10:15 p.m.

The posole was wonderful. Mick served it with fried plantains and a green salad, and we stuffed ourselves while kicking around ideas about the case. All three of us were entertaining serious doubts as to the existence of Davis Segretti.

Mick said, "What I've come up with is exactly nothing: no photographs, no academic records, no driver's or other licenses, no passport, no network of friends and associates, no professional associations, no insurance or property records, no bank or brokerage accounts. WHS—the company that holds the deed on the Rowan Court house—is a tough nut to crack. They conceal assets nationwide; we'll need a real power broker to get into their files."

I knew a fair amount about asset concealment from other cases the agency had handled. Wealthy persons and entities that wish to avoid paying income taxes devise many ingenious ways to minimize their taxable net worth, such as offshore and foreign accounts and dummy corporations. The shields of secrecy around such arrangements are extremely difficult to breach.

I said to Mick, "I assume you'll be working on locating someone who can get into those files."

"Yes, ma'am."

Hy shook his head. "Who would want to invent a person like Davis Segretti? To have a nonexistent entity to blame something on? And for what?"

I shrugged. "It's really too soon to tell. Were you able to get anything on Theo Segretti?"

"She's almost as much of a blank page as her supposed husband."

"But at least we've seen her in the flesh."

"Or someone purporting to be her."

The three of us fell glumly silent.

I said, "I'll try talking with Theo again tomorrow, but I doubt I'll get much farther with her than we already have."

"The first time you went up to the house, didn't she say something about a maid?" Hy asked.

"The maid. Yes. She was supposed to be sleeping in the servants' quarters, and Theo said she'd be all right since— what was her name?—Benicia Angelos was there. Maybe I should try to talk with her."

Hy shook his head. "Theo's probably warned her about you. Do we know somebody who's bilingual and good at chatting up strangers?"

"Julia."

"She's just getting acclimated from being off on leave."

"Anybody else?" Mick asked.

Hy and I both said, "Rae."

While I briefed Rae about what we hoped she could find out from Benicia Angelos, Hy and Mick got into the brandy. By the time I joined them they were mellow.

Mick asked me, "Do you ever think of Grandma Katie?"

The question surprised me. Katie McCone, my adoptive mother, had been gone a few years now. "There's never a day when I don't think of her—Ma was not someone you're ever likely to forget."

Mick smiled fondly. "Remember her big pilgrimage?"

I smiled too. About the time I met Hy, my mother had embarked on a journey to visit each of her adult children in order to explain why she was divorcing our father. Pa had never been the most attentive of husbands, either being gone at sea during his career as a US Navy chief or puttering in the garage while singing bawdy ballads during his retirement. Ma had met Melvin Hunt at one of the coin-operated laundries he owned (Pa had neglected to fix her washer for six months) and fallen in love with, as she'd put it, "a man who can get something done."

"She was happy with Melvin," Mick said.

"Yes, and even after he died, she was happy living on the Monterey Peninsula and selling her watercolors. They're considered quite collectible now."

"I cried when she died."

"Me too."

Mick seemed in the mood to reminisce. "I don't think Grandpa even cared that she'd left him."

"Well, he had his woodworking hobby." He'd died in his workshop fitting together the pieces of a box he was making for me. I'd been informed of his heart attack in the midst of the reception after Rae and Ricky's wedding and kept the news to myself until they'd left to catch their flight for their Paris honeymoon.

"Neither Ma nor Pa wanted you to know you were adopted."

"Actually, Pa did want me to find out. He put it in his will that I was to clear out his stuff, where he kept my adoption papers." I'd been devastated, gone on a search for the family who'd given me up, and found much more than I'd bargained on.

Saskia Blackhawk, who had conceived me during a one-night stand when she was an impoverished student, was now a Native-rights attorney who had successfully argued for our people before the US Supreme Court. My father, Elwood Farmer, was a nationally acclaimed painter living on the Blackfoot Indian Reservation in Montana. I also had siblings from Saskia's later marriage—a half sister, Robin Blackhawk, now an attorney in Los Angeles, and a half brother, Darcy Blackhawk, who was mentally disturbed and drug addicted. So far the only way the family had found to help him was to move him to various facilities around the country, where he continually wore out his welcome.

Well, as Hy frequently told me, no family's perfect. I'd found acceptance and affection from Saskia, Elwood, and Robin, as well as my "symbolic cousin" Will Camphouse. Will and I had met on the reservation, where I'd gone to visit Elwood; Native bloodlines being as confused and undocumented as they frequently are, we'd never been able to figure out if we were actually related, so we'd opted for symbolic status. Will, now owner of an ad agency in Seattle, had remained a friend. Evidence of our closeness was the number of times he'd tried to help the family out in our struggles with Darcy.

As if he could read my thoughts, Mick asked, "Where's Darcy now?"

"Someplace called Wellwood Manor in Nebraska. He's been there six months now, so we're hoping the treatment program there is working."

"Moving east, is he?"

"Yeah. We're hoping someplace works out before we hit the Atlantic."

"He's kind of a sweet guy, though, isn't he?"

"He can be, when he's not in a paranoiac rage. I don't want to discuss him any longer."

Mick said, "Well, how about the rest of our family? I haven't heard from Uncle John since I moved. And I never hear from Aunt Patsy. I thought she was getting married."

"John's busy expanding Mr. Paint into Arizona." My brother was a successful contractor. "And Patsy didn't get married—again. But she's opening another restaurant, this one in Novato." My youngest sister had three children, each by a different father. She'd managed to slip the bonds of matrimony within days of each planned wedding.

Mick smiled. "Doesn't surprise me. At least she's moving closer to us all the time. But Shar, who would've thought the McCone family would become so successful?"

I smiled. "None of our high school teachers, that's for sure."

We ended the evening on that happy note.

SUNDAY, NOVEMBER 6

7:55 a.m.

On the phone, Derek's voice was light and cheerful, as if he'd had an exceptionally good night's sleep.

"Shar," he said now, "I've got something for you."

"Unh." I pushed hair off my forehead, propped myself up on one elbow.

"Bad time to call?"

"No. What have you got?"

"A distant relative for Sam Sage. I was going over the files again and spotted the name. Was lost in all the clutter."

Too much data. Sometimes I feel like I'm swimming in it.

"Who's this relative?"

"A second cousin: James Kilburn. Lives in a place called Gray's Landing. Little town south of Red Bluff."

"You have contact information?"

He read it off to me.

"I'll check it out and get back to you."

I got up, went to my laptop. Gray's Landing was a quiet, rural location. Might be a good place for Sam to hide. I dialed the number Derek had given me. It was no longer in service.

It would be a long drive up there, and chances were nobody would be in residence. Flying, however...

I went to AirNav.com. The Red Bluff Municipal Airport was two miles south of town and offered parking in tie-downs. Public transportation was limited, but there was a car rental service nearby and numerous motels in case I needed to stay the night. I called the car rental office and asked if they would pick up at the airport. Yes, indeed. The agent sounded glad to hear of prospective business.

Local maps: I accessed two; nothing in Gray's Landing would be difficult to find. My mind made up, I threw a few things into a small travel bag and woke Hy.

"I'm going to take the plane for a while, maybe overnight," I told him.

He frowned, as if I were speaking in a strange tongue.

"You don't need it, do you?" I added.

"Right now I couldn't tell how to start it, much less fly it." He and Mick had sat up drinking brandy long after I went to bed.

I said, "Well, enjoy your day of rest. I'll call later."

8:48 a.m.

We'd fueled Two-Seven-Tango, our Cessna 170B, after the last time we flew, so preflighting was fast and soon I was airborne, heading northeast into the watery morning sunlight. The Bay and then the East Bay suburbs quickly faded behind me. The Sacramento River narrowed to a thin blue channel; I skirted the sprawl of the state capital and flew steadily over thick forest and then grassland that had been left gray brown by the summer and fall heat. Sparse herds of cattle moved slowly over the hillocks. Hawks wheeled high in the sky.

Red Bluff Municipal Airport was a paved field not far out of town with no traffic at present. A voice on the UNICOM directed me to the visitor tie-downs, where six or seven small planes stood. I landed, fighting a mild crosswind, and a few minutes later a ponytailed young woman in an old orange Jeep showed up and helped me secure the plane.

"I'm Emmy from Econocar," she told me. "The Jeep's your rental, and you can drop me by the lot on your way out. Got a place to stay?"

"Not yet."

"Try the Golden Hills. It's the best in town." She flashed me a toothy grin. "Of course, I say that because it belongs to my brother-in-law."

"Sounds good. Do I need a reservation?"

"Oh no. This is our slow time of year."

I thanked her, dropped her off, and followed the map I'd copied off the internet to Gray's Landing.

The countryside was as desolate as it had looked from the air: vast swaths of dead grasses, occasional jagged outcroppings, tumbledown fencing and barns. I tried to picture the land as it might be in a normal spring, the fields green and vibrant with wildflowers, but the image failed to materialize.

There were no signs of life until the town appeared, and few of them there either. The old buildings were wood or fake adobe, most of the storefronts dusty or papered over, a few with windows that had been smashed and taped up. A fifties-style movie theater whose marquee claimed it was the home of the First Pentecostal Church looked as if it hadn't hosted services in years. A pair of old men sat on a bench outside a drugstore, but the passage of a strange vehicle didn't provoke their attention. I slowed beside a school with unused playing fields and looked at my map again. I turned left, back into the countryside.

What did people do in a place like this? I wondered. There were few shops, no restaurants except for a closed-up lunch counter, no movie theaters, not even a bowling alley. Most of the small homes were topped by satellite dishes; maybe TV was the citizens' sole source of entertainment.

Orchards grew right up to the ditch beside the road: apples, I thought, and maybe walnuts. The home belonging to James Kilburn, Sam Sage's second cousin, was at the far end of a lane that wound off the highway between more groves, with a driveway that ended in a turnaround in front. A FOR SALE sign was propped against its mailbox.

I pulled the Jeep up in the dooryard and got out. Silence, except for the far-off screeching of crows. The house was wood frame with blistered white paint; dead flower beds hugged its porch, and rosebushes raised gnarled fists against the front windows. I went up on the porch, avoiding a missing step, looked for a bell push, and finally used the rusty knocker. A hollow, nobody-home sound echoed within.

The property also contained a small barn and two mostly collapsed sheds. On one side of the house were the remains of a vegetable garden; on the other was a chicken coop, but no sign of chickens. No sign, either, of Sam Sage's white truck. Maybe in the barn...

I crossed to the barn, my feet crunching on the gravel. Its double doors were fastened with a hasp but no padlock.

I called out in case someone was inside, and when I got no answer, I pulled the doors apart and poked my head into the gloomy interior.

Empty. A few rusted tools—rakes, shovels—hung on the wall. No hay in the loft. There were three horse stalls, their sides collapsing in on one another.

I went back to the house, found a rear door. Locked. I raised my arm to the dusty window and rubbed the pane with my sleeve. Peered inside. The door opened into a mudroom, where a couple of jackets hung on hooks. A light shone from a low-wattage bulb hanging on a bare cord from the ceiling.

Somebody here recently? Somebody who'd left a light on during the day? And one of the jackets, with the faux-leather patches on the elbows, looked familiar. Sam's? It resembled what he'd been wearing when I'd talked with him at his place in the city.

I left the barn and retraced my steps to the front of the house. Looked at the Realtor's sign and then called the number on it. A perky voice said I'd reached Colleen Dolan and asked me to leave a message. Sunday was a busy time for Realtors, I guessed, even in this backwater. I left my cell in the Jeep while I extended my search of the property.

After crossing some twenty yards of weedy, sloping ground, I came to a grove of gnarled apple trees. Windfalls littered the ground, and the smell of rotting fruit was strong. Tire tracks had gouged a deep groove in the ground between them, as if a vehicle had been driven through recently. A hawk circled lazily above and let out a shrill cry before spiraling away. As I moved into the grove, I could hear water running close by. In spite of the gurgling water, the silence was oppressive. Nothing—not a leaf or a twig—moved.

Something is very wrong here.

The sudden feeling was strong enough to make me reach into my bag for my .38. Tension built between my shoulder blades, as it always did when I found myself in a potentially dangerous situation. The instinct had seldom lied.

I kept moving forward, following the ruts, holding the .38 inside the bag. Still nothing to see or hear. The apple trees grew closer together here, and a broken lower branch on one of them tore at my clothing, scratched at my face and hands. I wasn't paying enough attention to the ground, tripped in one of the ruts, and went down on my knees. Pushed up, brushing dirt from my jeans.

The sound of water was louder now, rushing and splashing as it battered against an obstacle. It came from off to my right. The tire tracks veered that way, and so did I. When I came out of the grove, I could see a narrow creek swollen with rain runoff, a frothy wake on its surface where the sky-gray current diverged around a large white object—

It was a pickup truck, its bed tipped up and its cab half-submerged.

Sam's truck? Where was he?

I scrambled along the tire tracks and waded into the stream. It wasn't more than knee deep at first, then dropped off gradually; by the time I reached the truck, I was up to my waist in chilly water. I clung to the bed, pulled myself along to the cab on the driver's side. The truck was canted over on the passenger side, and the driver's-side window was rolled down. I stood on tiptoe to peer inside—

He was in there, on the passenger seat, most of his body

submerged. His head lolled with the current that flowed around him. His eyes were open in a ghastly parody of surprise, and when I reached in to touch his face, he felt colder than the swirling current.

Sam Sage hadn't died by drowning, though. There was a bullet hole smack in the middle of his forehead.

1:55 p.m.

I'd left him there for the investigating officers, dragged myself up the bank and across the yard to the decrepit house, fetched my cell from the Jeep, and called for help. Squad cars from the sheriff's department and the state highway patrol were now parked helter-skelter in the dooryard, the officers bunched together, presumably squabbling over jurisdiction. I'd spoken with them briefly and now sat on the steps of the house, wrapped in a blanket one of the officers had kindly provided and talking with Colleen Dolan, the real estate agent who had arrived shortly after the others. She'd come in response to my message.

"I didn't really know Mr. Kilburn," she told me. "He picked my name out of an ad in the Red Bluff paper and asked me to come out and take a look at his home. He wanted me to sell it as is, because he was going into a nursing home up there, the Shady Grove. That was six months ago. I advertised for a while and only got one lowball offer from a developer. When Mr. Kilburn countered, the developer bowed out."

"Did Mr. Kilburn ever mention his second cousin Sam Sage?"

"As far as I knew, he had no family."

"When was the last time you were out here?"

"Six weeks ago, maybe seven."

"Was everything in working order?"

"Yes. I checked the house and the outbuildings. Nothing had been touched."

"Was the electrical service on?"

"Electrical service, yes. My firm had seen to that, for security's sake. Minimal heat and no phone, however. I guess it'll be up to me to notify Mr. Kilburn of what happened here."

"Probably the police or sheriff's office will want to talk with him."

She glanced skeptically at the huddle of officers. "I think I'd better go ahead and contact him. It doesn't look as if one hand knows what the other's doing over there." She stood, gave me her card, and walked off toward her gray Acura. The officers didn't notice her departure.

I shivered and pulled the damp blanket closer. The pale shafts of sunlight had slipped behind cloud cover that brought the smell of rain, and wind stirred the grasses at my feet. I was about to go to my rental Jeep for a pair of dry socks when a sheriff's deputy motioned to me.

"Ms. McCone," he said, "I'd like you to come into the substation with me to give a statement."

So the investigation had been determined to be in the hands of the county.

I stood. "I'll follow you in my vehicle."

"Very well." His expression was wary, though. What, did he think I was going to flee the scene in my soggy shoes and clothing? Fortunately, he allowed me to retain his departmental blanket.

3:37 p.m.

My statement, given to Deputy Sheriff Bud Wentz, took a long time as his personnel wandered in and out of the small interview room, some of them seeming to have no more pressing business than to view the private investigator from the big city. I admit I looked a pretty sorry specimen with my lank hair and stained clothing and the collection of bruises—which I'd sustained banging into the submerged truck—that had started to emerge on my face and arms. When we were wrapping things up, I asked a clerk to call the Golden Hills Motel for an overnight reservation. No way was I in any shape to fly home tonight.

The Golden Hills had an A-frame façade and a low-slung attached coffee shop. Emmy from Econocar had already briefed its proprietor on my arrival, and he showed me to a room at the back of the central courtyard. "Very quiet, Ms. McCone. I guarantee it." I believed him; with the exception of a couple of big rigs parked near the coffee shop, the place was deserted.

I dragged my small bag in, shed my clothes, and took a long, hot shower. Then I lay down on the bed and called Hy, told him where I was and how I'd found Sam Sage's body.

"So what happened here?" Hy asked. "Sage told you he was going to 'take the money and run.' What money?"

"I guess from his meth operation. But from what the SFFD inspectors have determined, he wasn't cooking all that much meth. Certainly not enough for him to make the kind of profit that would be a major reason to flee town."

"Other money, then. And a large enough amount that he would've risked apprehension to salvage it. But how much and from what? And if he had it with him, what happened to it?"

"Maybe he hid it in the old house. Or it was in the truck and it's now rotting at the bottom of the river or floating toward the Golden Gate." I sighed. "Well, it's a police matter now. Let them look for it and figure out where it's from."

"Another big question," Hy said. "How did the murderer know where Sam was hiding?"

"Derek found the address, didn't he? He's not the only person to trace someone on the internet."

"True. But someone had to really want to find Sam to go to such lengths as to search for distant relatives."

"Someone determined and motivated."

"By what?"

"Could be anything. Revenge for a drug deal gone sour. Revenge for blackmailing or other dirty dealing. Sam was an internet scammer; maybe he got into something too big to handle."

I sighed. "And given the proliferation of scams, that could be anything."

Neither Hy nor I could guess at a satisfactory answer. Finally I asked him to inform Derek and Mick of what had happened and, when I couldn't doze after the call, began strategizing.

Contacting Sam Sage's second cousin in the nursing home didn't seem necessary. The real estate agent and sheriff's deputies would already have done so, and I could always get in touch with them should any questions occur to me. Better I should fly back home first thing in the morning. And then? More questioning of my contacts at the police and fire departments about the explosion at the Russian

Hill meth lab. In light of Sam's murder, that seemed the most likely line of investigation. And maybe Rae had had some luck with Theo Segretti's maid at Rowan Court.

My stomach growled. My God, I hadn't eaten since the pozole at Mick's nearly twenty-four hours earlier! I got up, tidied myself as best I could, and crossed the parking lot to the coffee shop, where I consumed a huge chicken-fried steak with all the trimmings.

MONDAY, NOVEMBER 7

1:11 p.m.

T here's definitely something not kosher about the situation at Rowan Court," Rae said.

We were sitting in the armchairs in the informal conversation section of my office at M&R, drinking Ted's good Sumatran blend of coffee from thick white mugs. Beyond the glass wall, the Bay lay flat and gray all the way to Alcatraz; beyond that, another wall of fog pressed in. Earlier I'd been concerned that the fog might hamper my landing at Oakland, but I'd slipped safely in before it thickened.

"How so?" I asked.

"The maid, Benicia Angelos, was very reticent with me. So reticent that I suspect she must be scared—not of me, but of her employers."

"Why don't you start at the beginning? How did you contact her?"

"I hung around that gatehouse until I saw the woman you described as Theo Segretti leave. She got into an Uber, and it went downhill toward Van Ness, so I figured she'd be gone awhile and went to the door. The maid, Benicia Angelos, is young—around eighteen, I'd guess—and very stylish. Passing out free magazines is a good way to get a housekeeper talking, and fortunately I had a recent copy of *Elle* in my briefcase, so I told her in Spanish that I was offering free subscriptions to fashion magazines and gave it to her. When I asked her if she was the lady of the house, she looked flattered and came out on the steps to talk. My Spanish, as you know, is limited, and when I admitted that, she switched to English. She's quite fluent, has only a slight accent."

"So you talked about...?"

"Fashion, at first. Benicia likes dressing up, says her employer gives her clothing she's only worn a time or two. I said her employer must be very kind, and maybe rich. Yes, she told me, Mrs. Segretti's clothes only come from the finest shops: Alexandre's, Piotor's, Les Artistes. No department stores or mail order for her."

"Do you know any of those places?"

"Well, sure. I shop at them all the time." She smoothed down her rumpled hoodie and jeans.

I raised my eyebrows.

"Well, I've *heard* of Alexandre's."

There was a tap at the door, and Ted entered with more coffee. He looked a lot better than he had during our conversation at my house. We hadn't had time to talk since then, and I wondered what was going on with him and Neal.

After he left, I said to Rae, "Go on about Benicia Angelos."

"Okay. Next I asked her if Mr. Segretti was proud of his wife's fashion sense. She looked confused. Mr. Segretti? I asked. The man of the house? She shook her head. I kept on after her: Mr. Segretti, he was gone a lot of the time, right? But that was okay, since he was making so much money to support his wife, no? Benicia then pretended to hear the phone ringing in the house and hurried inside, shutting the door on me."

"So we may be right in assuming there is no Mr. Segretti," I said. "And it's time to put a tail on Theo." I reached for the house phone, punched in Derek's extension, and gave him the particulars. He said he'd get someone on it.

"So what now?" Rae asked.

"We wait."

"Waiting's not in your nature. Or mine."

"No other choice."

So we waited, passing the time by grumbling about the state of our city.

"The way I see it," Rae said, "our number one problem is homelessness, and it's not going to be solved by the efforts of organizations like Ricky's and my foundation. We're working to get the city and state to step in with massive funding, and that's just not happening."

She was right, and in the meantime, tents were everywhere— and their inhabitants were the fortunate ones. Cardboard boxes were at a premium. Lines for city- and charity-run shelters stretched around blocks. People wrapped in tattered sleeping bags or rags sheltered under shrubbery or slept in the open. Many had come to California because of its reputation for a mild climate; nobody had told them of its blistering cold winters or—even during the drought— drenching rains.

I said, "What goes hand in hand with homelessness is drugs. Alcohol, of course, but also heroin, crack, opioids, meth, fentanyl, ecstasy, morphine—a lot of them diluted by pushers with other toxic substances."

Rae nodded. "There seem to be pushers on every corner. Used needles on all the sidewalks. People shuddering and dying in doorways—and most are too far gone to accept anyone's attempt to help them."

I was silent.

Rae asked, "You're thinking of Joey, aren't you?"

I nodded. Joey had been my older brother, the one between John and me. We hadn't been particularly close, in the way teenage brothers aren't with their bratty younger sisters. But both he and John and been kind, letting me hang out in the driveway and hand them tools while they tinkered with their dilapidated third- or fourth-hand cars. Then I'd gone away to college and heard little from him except for an occasional postcard from various places where he'd worked as a mechanic around northern California. Finally I'd gotten the call from my adoptive mother—the kind of call we all dread—saying that Joey had been found dead of an overdose in a shack in Eureka. I hadn't known that smiling, happy-go-lucky Joey was an addict, and it had taken me years to process the fact. Maybe I hadn't processed it yet—and never would.

To cover my rush of emotion, I said, "And then there's the crime rate. Fueled by too many guns."

In my opinion, the possession of illegal firearms was a cause for major nationwide concern. I'd owned several guns, although I preferred my old .38 Special. I was an excellent shot, practiced frequently at the range, and stored it in a safe place—usually the office safe. I was good with the idea of guns in the hands of qualified professionals who needed them; I was not good with the idea of them being in the hands of unqualified people who used them to support their egos. As more and more weapons that were only suited for battlefield situations continued to flood the market, I was increasingly concerned that our entire nation was turning into a battlefield.

Rae, who was also firearms qualified, said, "I can't imagine why any reasonable person wouldn't support gun control. Enough said on that subject. But here's another local problem: Have you been reading about the so-called Doom Loop?"

"You mean the idea that our downtown is on the verge of collapsing?"

"Yeah. Experts claim that if it does, the entire city will follow. Families will leave in droves, our tax base will be decimated, and our mass transit will be gutted. Some say it's the result of the pandemic. Folks working remotely, not going out and spending money. Which led to loss of jobs in the service industry, a high office vacancy rate, and the dot-com bust."

"You believe it's that bad?"

"Well, there have always been doomsayers, but in addition to them, locally we're contending with not-in-my-backyard attitudes. Nobody wants subsidized housing near them, nobody wants low-cost developments. Most of all, nobody wants a person they consider inferior or different living on their block. Nobody wants anything that doesn't fit their self-serving interests. Jesus, Shar, we're even dealing with crumbling seawalls. Now Aquatic Pier's been declared off-limits, is going to be demolished. Another symbol of our waterfront's history gone."

"Well, maybe we'll all be swept out into the ocean when the Big One hits!" I'd meant it as a joke, but it didn't come off as one.

Rae said, "This conversation is grim enough without getting into major earthquakes."

Mick rapped on the door and poked his head in. Our leisure time was over, thankfully.

"I've finally got some background on Theo Segretti," he announced.

He sat with us, began reading from his iPad. "She's an easterner from Salem, Mass—no jokes about witches, please. Birth name was Gifford. Attended local schools and a year at Bryn Mawr College. I suspect from the hesitancy of the woman I spoke with in the registrar's office there that Theo left under something of a cloud, but even the old Savage charm couldn't wring the details from her. Theo went home to Salem for a year and later to the University of Colorado Boulder, where she appears to have majored in playing pinball in local bars but managed to graduate with a BA in economics. She then took off with a boyfriend, Gilbert Jacoby, to Nevada City, where they ran a lucrative tourist shop and guide service. Jacoby reportedly moved back to Colorado three years ago, and Theo came down here alone and after a time ended up on Rowan Court."

"Nothing at all about the alleged husband, Davis?" I said.

"Nope. Not much doubt at this point that he doesn't exist and never did."

"What about her family? Anyone left in Salem?"

"Both parents are dead. Mother of cancer, five years ago. Father of a heart attack two years later. No siblings or other near relatives."

"She inherit anything?"

"No record of it."

"You sure there are no marriage records?"

"Yes. She never married Jacoby. I've put out an inquiry on him."

"Good. When did she start using the name Segretti?"

"When she came down here. She had a good deal of cash from the sale of the Nevada City business and took it to WHS, the asset management company, who control the place on Rowan Court."

"Interesting." I considered what he'd told us. "Well, we've put a surveillance on her and will just have to see what that turns up."

"Anything more for me?" he asked.

"Try to get a photo of this Jacoby. Start looking into WHS. And keep yourself available."

He flashed me a wry grin. "I'm always available these days."

When he left the office, Rae said, "He's not very happy, is he?"

"He puts a good face on it, but no."

"Needs a woman friend."

"He does. It's been a long time since he's seen anyone. That new place of his on Tel Hill—he's refurbished it all by himself, and it looks as if he's in for the long haul. And now there's our other bachelor—Ted." I explained about Neal and his wanderlust and Ted's desire for a permanent union.

"God, I'm glad all that uncertainty is behind me," she said.

"Me too."

We fell silent, reflecting. Hy and I were an old married couple by now, but I could still sense the wild streak in him—in me too. Rae and Ricky had settled, but his days of groupies and partying weren't all that far behind him.

And Rae—who knew where her imaginings took her as she wrote her novels?

"Enough," I said, standing. "I've got a pile of paperwork to plow through. We'll talk more later."

4:45 p.m.

Mick tapped on my office door. I gestured for him to come in, and he settled down in a client's chair, propping his booted feet on the corner of my desk. Mick is the only person I allow to do that—since it's unlikely he'll stop even if I insist.

He sailed a photograph across to me. "This is a picture of Gilbert Jacoby at a going-away party hosted for him by some of his buddies in Boulder last year."

I studied the photo. It showed a man with a long, narrow face topped with curly black hair. His eyebrows met in a straight line over the bridge of his nose, and one of those little chin patches that have become so popular curled down below thin lips. What struck me most was his eyes: dark and brooding, they seemed to bore into the viewer.

"Wouldn't want to meet up with him unarmed at close range," I said. "Where was he going away to?"

Mick shrugged. "I've got inquiries out to the Boulder pals, and I'm trying to establish a timeline on his activities after the party."

"I have a bad feeling about this. People connected to Theo Segretti have a tendency to disappear."

"You mean Sam Sage?"

"Right. And now Sage is dead. We'd definitely better tighten our surveillance on Segretti."

6:46 p.m.

Home with Hy, curled on the sofa in front of a crackling fire, drinking a good merlot and discussing the atmospheric river that was predicted to blow in from British Columbia during the night. The optimistic view was that the drought would be broken this winter, but I wasn't so sure. Many of the predicted rainstorms had failed to materialize, and much of the vegetation here at the Avila Street house was still brittle. We'd watered what plants looked to be in dire straits a week earlier, but now it looked as if they'd receive a much-needed soaking. I'd talked earlier to the caretaker for Touchstone, our property on the Mendocino Coast, and he'd told me winds there were high and a couple of old trees had come down, but the sea moisture was nurturing the others.

The Mendocino property was oceanfront, deeded to me years earlier by a grateful client who harbored bad memories of the place. It had consisted of a stone cottage on the cliff top and a rudimentary airstrip, and now a spacious home with a generous setback that had been hand built by Hy and a few of his contractor friends. We spent as much time as we could there, aided by internet access to our businesses.

We'd had another property once: the ranch near Tufa Lake in Mono County that Hy had inherited from his step-father. Two horses also: King Lear and Sidekick. But we'd gone there less and less, and the horses had preferred the ranch manager and his wife, Ramon and Sara Perez. Finally we'd sold the land to the Perezes to house their growing family. On a recent visit, we'd found the ranchhouse so much improved we were both ashamed of having let it deteriorate as it had. King and Sidekick still recognized us and nuzzled our hands as we fed them carrots. Of course, horses will *always* nuzzle a hand offering carrots...

We were discussing whether to order some kind of take-out when my cell rang. Jill Madison. I raised my eyebrows, said to Hy, "I'd better take this."

Her voice sounded tremulous. "Did you know Janus and Dino have been arrested?" Jill asked.

"Who...?" Oh, right—the menacing men in the turreted house at the end of her street on Bernal Heights. "On what charges?"

"Drugs. Selling cocaine or fentanyl, probably."

"When?"

"Late this afternoon. A neighbor down the street overheard what went on and told me."

"I'll have one of my operatives check with a connection at the department, let you know what the charges are and how long they'll be held in custody." I penciled a note to ask Mick.

"Wait!" A long pause on Jill's end of the line. I put my phone on speaker so Hy could hear. Finally she said, "I just heard something over there, sounded like breaking glass. Hold on a minute."

"Jill—"

But she was gone.

"Dammit," I said to Hy, "I hope she's not playing amateur detective again."

After a few minutes she came back on the line. "Somebody's in the house. There's a light on inside."

"Maybe Janus and Dino have been released."

"No, these aren't regular house lights. It's a flashlight moving around. Whoever it is must've broken in. I'm going over—"

"No! Stay where you are. Call the cops."

"They won't respond in time. They never do, not in this neighborhood."

"Call anyway." Hy was standing, putting on his jacket. He tossed me mine. I added, "And whatever you do, don't go over there."

"But whoever it is might get away—"

"Ripinsky and I will be there shortly."

She made a sudden excited sound. "Somebody's coming around from the back now. I'm gonna see where he goes." The line went dead.

"Dammit," I said as we headed for the door. "She's going to get herself in real trouble."

9:05 p.m.

I drove, steering the Miata through routes I knew well from having worked in the area for so long. We found Jill at the bottom of the lane, looking around frantically. She recognized my car and ran to it.

As I lowered my window, she said, "The guy that came out of the house hurried down the block, got into a car, and drove off."

"Did you get a good look at him?"

"Just enough to tell that he was big, wide shoulders, wearing a tan parka. The car was some foreign model; I've never seen it around here before. Gray maybe. He pulled a U-turn and took off. I got a partial plate number; it's—"

"Save it for the cops. You *did* call them?" I pushed her aside so I could get out.

"The lines were busy."

She was lying; she'd had plenty of time to get through on 911. Jill wanted to be the heroine of another investigation. I wondered if she'd made the whole thing up.

I said, "Get in this car and stay there. We'll be back."

"But—"

"Get in the car!" I shoved her into the driver's seat, nearly closed the door on her foot.

Hy and I started up the street. The bulb of the only streetlight on the court was out. The night was dark, the sky mostly overcast; the moon when it peeked out was a mere sliver through the bare tree limbs. The sound from the confluence of freeways below made a monotonous hum.

We drew close to the house. No lights showed inside that I could see as we moved around to the rear. A side window back there showed a faint light. Hy was already checking the load on his .45. I had my holstered weapon clipped to my belt within easy reach.

Next to the stairs a broken window yawned, shards of glass removed from its frame as if the intruder had taken care not to injure himself. Hy aimed his flashlight inside and flicked it on. The beam revealed a kitchen, massive curls of wallpaper peeling toward the floor. The appliances were eighties style—boxy and copper colored. A double sink was filled with piles of dirty dishes, and takeout containers and pizza boxes overflowed onto the worn linoleum floor.

A faint odor emanated from somewhere inside, overpowering the smell of rotted food. Hy recognized it as soon as I did and said the word in a tense whisper. "Kerosene."

He was about to boost himself through the window when a car with a heavy-duty engine came roaring up the rise. The cops? Or—? He switched off the flash and we both froze, listening. The car went past the house, then suddenly tires squealed on the pavement as the driver slammed on the brakes. There were more rubber-burning sounds, another engine roar that rapidly diminished. The driver had turned around. Not the cops—just somebody who'd probably taken a wrong turn and realized it when he spotted the NOT A THROUGH STREET sign.

Hy turned the flashlight back on and climbed through the broken window. I was right behind him. The reek of kerosene grew stronger as we went through the kitchen into a cluttered living room where a cornice had collapsed toward the fireplace, bisecting the space. On the far side a thin, pale light flickered—candlelight. We shoved our way around the cornice. On the floor a thick candle had been set into a box of shredded excelsior such as fragile items are packed in; more of the softwood shavings were spread out from it in half a dozen lines, like spokes on a wheel. All of it was doused in kerosene. And the candle flame was less than half an inch above the excelsior.

Hy acted quickly, stepping between the spokes to the box and pinching out the flame with his thumb and forefinger.

"Some damn fool's attempt at arson," he said. "We got here just in time."

"Do you suppose he set any others in the house?"

"We'd better check—and quickly."

There were no more arson setups in the other downstairs rooms.

A rickety staircase led to the second floor. The steps

creaked as we mounted them to a small hallway with three doors opening from it. The bathroom was clear, and the bedrooms contained only heaps of clothing and mattresses topped by sleeping bags.

The house had become oppressive, the intermingling stenches of garbage and kerosene making my head ache. I asked Hy, "You seen everything you want to?"

"Yeah. Let's get out of here."

On the way downstairs, I said, "I should've asked Derek or Mick to run a property check on this place, but at the time its ownership didn't seem important—just a squat in a bad neighborhood with a couple of guys running drugs out of it. Now we're looking at an arson attempt."

"And a damned amateur one at that. Another vandalism attempt?"

"Maybe not. The others have been...well, not exactly petty, but nothing on this scale. Could be this had something to do with the two squatters' drug activities—revenge for a deal gone bad."

"Could be. Or maybe whoever is responsible for the vandalisms is escalating their tactics."

"But why here, in this downscale neighborhood? I still don't see a connection with the other private streets. Or why that map was sent to me by way of Ted." A sudden thought occurred to me, one I should have had before. "Unless..."

"Unless what?"

I didn't answer. I was still focused on the thought.

We left the house the way we'd come in, through the broken kitchen window. The street was deserted—no police presence—and all the other dwellings were dark except for Jill's. She was no longer in my car.

"Must have gone back to her house," Hy said.

"She better have."

She had, and must have been watching the street through a window. She opened the door before I had a chance to knock. "I couldn't stay down in your car all alone," she said. "Too creepy."

"No problem. Did you try calling the police again?"

"Well... no. I just don't like cops."

"Let me have that partial plate number."

"I wrote it down for you." She handed me a piece of notepaper. I glanced at it, put it into my jacket pocket. I'd relay the number to Mick on the way home, along with the address of the turreted house, so he could search for ownership records.

I said, "You remember the first time I came here? I showed you a map that was left for me of this court?"

Her expression grew wary. "... Yes."

"You didn't really look at it."

"I looked—"

"Not closely. Because you'd seen it before."

"I'd seen..."

"Yes, you. When you drew it."

"No way!"

"Jill, you're a crime-solving junkie. You knew about the vandalisms on the private streets and the coalition hiring me before you even met me. And you contrived to meet me when you made the map and put it at my office manager Ted Smalley's home so he would bring it to my attention. I don't know how you got his address, but I assume you can find almost anything online."

She was silent.

"Your ploy worked," I went on. "A good part of my investigation's centered here now. But what have you really gained?"

Her expression grew conflicted. "Well, I'd hoped you would take me into your confidence, let me help you work the case. If I'd been in on it, I could've gotten great material for my blog, maybe used it for articles or even a book."

"You must've known that an investigator uses her own operatives and sources."

"I thought maybe you'd make an exception. I mean, I have a lot of good insights."

"Good insights? Look at what you've done. You used my office manager to bring your so-called insights to my attention. Did you wait around to see if he took your envelope to me, hoping to get my home address? That information isn't readily available—it's very closely protected."

She shrugged sullenly.

I went on, getting more and more angry as I ticked items off on my fingers. "You lied to me when I showed you the map, pretending you'd never seen it before. You deliberately misled me about what might be going on up here. You created a situation to arouse my suspicions when there was no real foundation for it. You dragged Hy and me out here late at night on a flimsy pretext. I wouldn't be surprised if, once you heard Dino and Janus were in jail, you set up this arson scene to draw even more attention to yourself."

"Arson? Is that what was going on over there? I don't know anything about it—I wouldn't know how to do that!"

"But if you had known, you might have."

"No, no way. I'm not a criminal, you know!"

"Certainly not. It was a very amateurish job."

"But not mine."

I didn't reply, regarded her stonily.

"Really," she said, "all I wanted to do was help you build a case."

"Against whom?"

"Well, maybe Dino and Janus? They're pretty bad guys."

"You have reason to believe they're involved in the vandalisms?"

"...No. They're just druggies with knives."

Mick had checked with the SFPD about the charges against the two; they had amounted to just that, no more.

"Okay, Jill," I said, "I'll let you go now."

"You mean you don't want to work with me?"

"I don't even want to *see* you again. You're a user, Jill. If you get over trying to latch on to a professional and decide you're still interested in pursuing a career in criminal justice, you should check out the offerings at City College."

She nodded, discouraged, and stepped back before closing the door on me.

TUESDAY, NOVEMBER 8

8:10 a.m.

Mick called to report that the turreted house on Herrera Court, and the gray 2017 Honda Civic Jill had seen leaving the property, belonged to Gwen Morgin, a co-owner of the Sedgwick Real Estate Company in the Inner Sunset. By his digital alchemy, he had pulled up a surprising bit of information. For one thing, Gwen Morgin was Gilbert Jacoby's sister.

"You can find out the damnedest things," I said, meaning it as a compliment.

"It's simple, if you take the trouble to look somebody up on WhosIt.com." He sounded annoyed that I hadn't done his work for him.

I was about to make a sharp retort—I wasn't feeling too cheerful myself this morning—but decided not to. He had a point, after all. I really shouldn't overload him and Derek with search requests I could take care of myself.

I drove out to Judah Street, where the Sedgwick Real Estate Company was housed in a nondescript tan stucco building near Eighteenth Avenue, N Judah streetcars rumbling past and shaking the ground like a mini earthquake.

Inside the office were lines of desks, most of them vacant. A slender woman with her brown hair in a ponytail was the only visible occupant. I asked if Gwen Morgin was in, and she told me Ms. Morgin was out showing a property. Would I care to wait?

"Actually, it's Ms. Morgin's brother, Gilbert Jacoby, who I'm trying to locate."

The woman's nostrils flared in distaste. "Ah, yes. Gil. He was in yesterday, looking over our low-end rental listings here in the Avenues, but apparently they cost more than he wants to pay."

"So he didn't actually view any of the properties?"

"I think Gwen may have shown him one or two. There was a bungalow on Thirty-Sixth Avenue and a flat on Forty-First that we've had listed for a while. Do you want me to check and see if either's been rented?"

"Please."

She went into a cubicle toward the rear. "You're in luck," she told me when she returned brandishing a sheet of paper. "The bungalow on Thirty-Sixth was rented yesterday, and the notation is in Gwen's writing."

I pocketed the paper and turned to go.

"Oh!" she exclaimed. "Just a minute. Here's Gwen now."

Gwen Morgin resembled her brother: stocky, with heavy shoulders and long dirty-blond hair. She wore a beige pant-suit that looked a size too small and large hoop earrings made of varicolored plastic. As she walked toward us, she teetered on the kind of stiletto heels that—unfortunately for wearers' spines—have come back into fashion.

Her colleague introduced me and went to the only desk outfitted for work. "So," Morgin said, "what is it?"

I guessed I didn't look like a prospect. "Are you the owner of the house"—I consulted the address I'd noted down—"at thirteen Herrera Terrace?"

"Yeah. What of it?"

"Somebody attempted to burn it down last night."

She paled and set her purse on the nearest desk. "That can't be. I would've heard."

"I said *attempted.* The fire was extinguished."

"Still, I would've heard. The fire department would've called me."

"They didn't extinguish it."

"Then who— Wait, who're you?"

I handed her my card.

She stared blankly at it, then said, "What business is it of yours?"

"I'm one of the parties who extinguished it."

"Jesus." She pulled out the desk chair and sat.

"Do you know who might have wanted to burn your house down?"

"Not the guys who are squatting there. I pay them to make sure nobody bothers it."

That was a surprise. "You *pay* Janus and Dino? How much?"

"Just a little, plus some—"

"Some what?"

She made a feeble gesture and pressed her hand to her forehead.

"Some drugs?" I pressed.

"When I've got them. I don't care about the house—I just want to keep it standing till I can cash in. That property's gonna be worth a lot soon."

"Why?"

"Everything appreciates sooner or later."

I switched to another tack. "What about your brother, Ms. Morgin?"

"Gil? What about him?"

"Why didn't you install him there to keep it safe?"

"Shit! Do I look like an idiot? I wouldn't let him near *any-thing* I own. The man's a parasite. Tried to move in on me here, but I couldn't take it, threw him out. Managed to get him into a cheap house we had listed and loaned him my car to move his trailer there. I bet he's already trashed the place. He's a slob and a user. I've helped him out of enough scrapes in my life. No way I'm dealing with him again."

"What cheap house is that, Ms. Morgin?"

She shook her head. "You want to find him, you go right ahead. You're the detective."

10:35 a.m.

Judging from the other real estate agent's reaction, I thought as I drove farther into the Avenues, Gilbert Jacoby didn't inspire much liking in those he met. The photograph Mick had given me tended to suggest why: the sneer, the hard eyes, the jutting jaw all indicated a hostile, perhaps dangerous, attitude toward the world around him.

An unhitched U-Haul trailer was pulled up across the driveway of a small clapboard house on Thirty-Sixth Avenue, but no one was unloading it. I checked the address, then parked behind the van. A padlocked chain held the rear doors shut. The wooden stairway leading to the house's entrance wobbled beneath me as I climbed them; I knocked three times and heard heavy footsteps approaching from within.

"Yeah?" a rough voice called out. The door opened and I was suddenly face to face with Gilbert Jacoby. He was greatly changed from the photograph taken of him in Denver: many pounds heavier, puffy cheeks stubbled, eyes reddened, chin patch untrimmed. He wore a stained work shirt, ripped jeans, and running shoes that had seen more than the average number of miles.

"Who're you?" he demanded.

I handed him my card.

He glanced at it, then crumpled it and threw it to the ground. "You're the bitch they was telling me about. You're not coming in here."

Making an effort to keep my voice even, I said, "Who's been telling you about me, Mr. Jacoby?"

"None of your business." He moved to shut the door.

I stuck out my foot to prevent it from closing. "It couldn't be Janus and Dino. They don't know me."

"Who?"

"The men in the house at the end of Herrera Court."

Hesitation. Then, "What court?"

"Herrera. On Bernal Heights. Above Coso."

"I don't know what you're talking about."

"The house with the turrets. The one owned by your sister. An arson fire was set there last night—kerosene-soaked excelsior and a lighted candle. I think you're the one who did it."

His glance shifted—left, right, left. It gave me a chance to peer inside the house: no other person to back him up, nothing but a few furnishings and unpacked boxes.

"You're crazy. It wasn't me."

"It was you, all right. You were seen leaving the place and driving away in your sister's car. And I can smell the kerosene on you." He was sweating now, and that kind of fuel takes a while to wash off; it gets into the pores. The faint odor was on his clothes too. He hadn't bothered to change them.

"I never burned down no goddamn house."

"It didn't burn down. My associate and I got there in time to prevent it."

He didn't say anything. There was a scared, guilty look in his shifty eyes.

"Why did you do it? Some kind of trouble with the two druggies who lived there?"

He shook his head.

"Did somebody pay you for the torch job?"

"No…"

"Come on, Jacoby." No more "Mr." now. "Who told you to torch that house? Your sister, maybe?"

"My sister! That bitch would never—"

"She owns the house. And it was her car you were driving last night."

"She let me use the car, yeah, but that's all. She threw me out of the house she lives in. She deserved to get the other one torched."

"So you tried that just to get even. She didn't know anything about it."

He was silent, his arms folded across his chest.

"And it wasn't connected to the other vandalisms."

He said too quickly, "What vandalisms?"

"You know damn well what vandalisms, Jacoby. You're the one responsible for them."

"The hell I am."

"The hell you're not." I took out my cell phone and held it up. "You can talk to me about them and who put you up to them, or you can have a lot more trouble with the police. Vandalism is a misdemeanor, but attempted arson is a serious felony."

The fight went out of him suddenly, as it sometimes does with big, blustery guys confronted by someone they think is in authority. He looked mean and tough, but he wasn't. He was weak and cowardly, in addition to not being very bright.

"All right, I did that stuff. But it wasn't much, just a couple of little jobs to pick up some quick cash."

"A *couple*?"

"Well, three."

"Try four."

"Okay, five. Whatever. I don't remember exactly, my memory's not so good these days."

"One of them was the brush fire on Russian Hill, near where the meth lab blew up."

"Meth! Jesus Christ! I don't know nothing about meth."

"You know Sam Sage?"

"Who?"

"He lived up there and was cooking the meth. He's dead now. Murdered."

"Murdered? Jesus!"

"The person who paid you for the vandalisms must have told you about him. Your old partner, Theo Segretti."

A muscle jumped on his cheek, making the corner of his mouth twitch.

"Well, Jacoby?"

"Yeah. Yeah, all right, it was Theo. But it wasn't supposed to be that way."

"Which way?"

"Her and me, we had a good business up north. Then

these guys offered her a job down here, and she sold the business out from under me and left."

"What guys?"

"I don't know, she wouldn't say. Told me I couldn't be part of it, that I wouldn't fit in."

"Part of what?"

"Whatever they wanted her for. Theo, she's smart, knows a lot about a lot of things. Something about land...yeah, land trusts is what she called it."

"But you came down anyway."

"Yeah. We had a pretty good time when it was just the two of us running the wilderness guide business, but she got tired of that. Wanted something more sophisticated, was how she put it. I wasn't having any of that nonsense, so I followed her, stayed with my sister, found the place Theo had moved to. Living pretty damn high, she is. So I got in touch with her, and she said she'd give me jobs to do, help me to rent a place of my own."

"And you took her up on it."

"I needed the money. My damn sister won't have me with her."

"Theo told you exactly which streets to vandalize, including the one she lived on?"

"Yeah, but not why. I couldn't get that outta her." He blinked as if struck by a thought. "Hey, she didn't have anything to do with what's-his-name, Sam Sage, getting killed, did she?"

"I don't know. She may have."

"Ah, Christ." Then he said, his voice turning whiny, "Listen, what happens now? To me, I mean. You gonna have me arrested?"

"What do you think?"

"I think I'm outta here." He dodged backward and slammed the door so hard it shook the whole porch. I could hear him thundering toward the rear of the house. On his way to see Segretti or to try leaving the city? Anyway, we had most exits covered. The damn fool wouldn't get far.

11:55 a.m.

As I drove back downtown, I called Hy and gave him a quick outline of what I'd learned from Jacoby. He said he'd alert the operatives surveilling Theo Segretti in case Jacoby showed up on Rowan Court.

"You want the police in on this yet?" he asked.

"No. We need more information on who Segretti's working with, what that land trust business is all about, and more direct evidence about the vandalisms. Has Mick found out anything about that firm Segretti is associated with—WHS?"

"Yeah, and you're not going to like it. He finally managed to get a list of the members of their board of directors. You know one of them—Glenn Solomon."

I drew in my breath. "Damn!"

Glenn—one of the state's most prominent criminal defense attorneys. My former friend, former nemesis. My now...what?

Over the years, Glenn and I had sparred about various issues concerning my investigations of cases involving his clients. Some of his complaints had been minor, others major—including a direct interference on his part that had nearly cost me my life. But at other times we'd been amiable, if not the best of buddies.

"You two on the ins these days or on the outs?" Hy asked.

"I think things're copacetic. Anyway, it's best I have a talk with him."

"But will he talk with *you*?"

"He will—I'll see to that."

"God help him!"

Glenn, I knew, had built a solid wall of gatekeepers around him, but he was also a creature of habit. With that in mind, I went to the agency, where my day was filled with paperwork and conferences with operatives—from both my side of the firm and Hy's. Since we'd merged our operations, our individual caseloads had expanded, although my side was largely concerned with domestic matters while his still handled international affairs and executive protection. Each of us, however, needed to know the full scope of our operations, and we were both hands-on administrators— which meant long hours absorbing information. Sometimes I wonder why we're both so diligent about it, but we never know when a certain seemingly minor fact can take on great significance to either one of us.

Finally, four o'clock rolled around. Gil Jacoby had not shown up at Segretti's house, one of the ops reported to Hy, and she was no longer there. She'd gone down to Van Ness, where she had a car, a pale-green Volvo, garaged and driven to the Bay Bridge, where she'd managed to lose the ops tailing her in a traffic tie-up. So much for that situation. I packed up my remaining files and drove down the waterfront to Embarcadero Center to visit Glenn.

The center is a five-building high-rise commercial complex anchoring the northwest corner of our waterfront. Developed between 1971 and 1989, it houses offices, retail establishments, restaurants, entertainment venues, hotels, and even a skating rink. A city unto itself, if a rather sterile one.

As I reached the doors of Solomon Associates on the top floor of Embarcadero Three at exactly five o'clock, they opened, and Glenn breezed through, as I'd known from past experience that he would, on his way to his favorite watering hole, Rosanna's, on the thirty-first floor.

Glenn was in his late seventies, although he looked much younger. A big bear of a man, he sported a thick mane of white hair and was always impeccably attired. His bright blue eyes twinkled when he saw me.

"Sharon McCone! You spending a lot of time hanging out around elevators these days?" he asked.

"Only when looking for a special friend. That is, if we *are* friends."

He pretended to consider, his brows knitting together. "These days—yes. Come with me, and I'll serve you a special libation."

He ushered me back into the office suite and seated me in a conversation circle near one of the huge windows overlooking the downtown district. A snap of his fingers brought a young man with a bar cart. "Two Solomon's specials," he told the man. To me he added, "Josh here is Harvard Law; he put himself through as a bartender and volunteers for the duty when I'm serving special guests."

More likely he'd been coerced into it with the promise of future advancement.

Josh poured the premixed drinks into tall glasses. Solomon's specials were vodka laced with a varying assortment of liqueurs—the more exotic the better, in his opinion. *Sip slowly*, I warned myself.

Glenn settled back and sighed contentedly. "A perfect end to a not-so-perfect day. Besides your fondness for me, I suspect you're here for information about WHS Asset Management."

The man could still surprise me. "How did you know?"

"Their tracking devices indicate inquiries from your office."

"Very sophisticated." I'd have to warn Mick to set his antidetection levels higher.

Glenn asked, "What's your interest in the firm?"

"Generally how it works."

"And specifically?"

"About a property—maybe more than one—that it manages for a person who's come up in one of my investigations."

"What property is that?"

"A parcel on Rowan Court here in the city."

"I see." Glenn pursed his lips thoughtfully.

"The individuals occupying the property are Theresa and Davis Segretti."

"And of what transgressions are they guilty?"

"Sorry, Glenn—confidential."

"Yet you want *me* to break confidentiality."

"I'm willing to trade."

He smiled, shaking his head. "A swap meet, eh?"

"Of sorts. I can repay you in the future."

"All right." He reached for a laptop lying on the coffee table in front of us and brought up a file. "Allow me a few moments; I haven't looked at this in a long time."

After a bit he said, "WHS Asset Management—full name Whitten, Holst, and Severance. Was established in 1972, and the original partners are all deceased. Primary shareholders are Winslow Lambert and Benjamin Aspirillo, both of San Francisco."

I wasn't familiar with the name Benjamin Aspirillo, but Winslow Lambert sounded familiar...Oh, right—the deposed director of the now-defunct People for Equitable Housing.

"Asset management firms," Glenn continued, "as you may or may not know, handle legitimate transactions for their clients: purchases and sales of stocks and bonds, real estate, and such. But there are those who use their skills to outwit the IRS and other fiduciary agencies. WHS is known for its skill in those areas."

"And you're on the board of such a corporation?"

Glenn shook his head, smiling slightly. "Nominally on the board, and don't give me that chiding look, Sharon. You've been around long enough to recognize the shady from the *truly* shady activities. I allowed a few clients to place me in a position where I could supervise certain transactions; over the years I've saved them a world of grief."

Kept them out of prison too, I bet.

I said, "So tell me about Davis and Theresa Segretti."

"I have no knowledge of them."

"Glenn..."

"But I do have knowledge of someone who does."

I waited.

"This is not going to please you. It strikes too close to home. Tell me: Who put you on to this case initially?"

"The Coalition for the Preservation of Private Streets."

"That's fine. But someone had to make you aware of them and their problem. Who was that individual?"

"Derek Frye, an operative who heads our research department. His father, Martin Frye, recommended I contact them."

"There you are."

"I don't understand."

"Then you'd best ask Mr. Frye. And hope that you're not further deceived."

7:00 p.m.

I'd called Derek immediately after leaving Embarcadero Center and asked him to meet me at the agency at seven. He was already there when I arrived, in his office with spreadsheets on the desktop before him. He wasn't studying them, however; his hands were clasped, his eyes focused on the lights of the distant East Bay hills. Tension stretched the cords of his neck, straining the ornate snake tattoo that circled them.

From the doorway I said, "Glenn Solomon called and warned you I wanted to talk, didn't he?"

Derek cleared his throat but didn't turn to look at me. "Not Glenn. He called my father. And my father called me."

I should have known. No matter how much friendship one of the members of the old boy business network professed to an outsider like me, they remained true to their own.

"And what did your father instruct you to do?"

"Frankly, to lie."

"Are you going to?"

"No, I'm not."

I went into the room, took one of the client chairs across the desk from him.

After a moment, Derek made and maintained eye contact. "I've told you about the difficulties of my relationship with my father."

"Yes." He had, a few years earlier, and had seemed to regret it. We'd never spoken of it since, but the strictures

Martin Frye had placed upon Derek had remained a serious point of contention between father and son, and I gathered it had only grown as time went by.

"It weighs on me, Shar," Derek said now. "Here I am, a grown man, but always held in contempt by the old man. He's vocal about not respecting me or my work here at the agency. He refers to my creative endeavors like SavageFor as 'trivial fun and games.' And now this latest demand that I go around my loyalty to you—it's unconscionable."

"Explain the demand."

"I'm to keep him informed on every detail of this private-streets case and turn over copies of all the relevant files to him. In return, he'll release my trust and let me go my own way. If I don't, he'll make a new will and void the trust."

"That trust—how much is it worth by now?"

Derek shrugged. "Seventy, eighty million. I haven't kept up on it. The thing is, the money's never seemed real to me. Or mattered much."

"Any other demands?"

"To say that he never contacted me about the case. I'm to say none of your findings are correct. He wants me to claim that the whole investigation is baseless, a publicity stunt on M&R's part."

"Did he give any indication as to who's orchestrating this? Because there has to be somebody very powerful to force him to make demands like these."

"My father doesn't give reasons, Shar. He's a reason unto himself."

But Martin Frye wasn't the ultimate reason. He was powerful, but this demand went way up the power chain. I thought of what Hy had said about power: "Corporate. City.

State. National. International. You name it, it's out there, and everybody's after it."

"Derek," I said, "Who can you think of who could coerce your father into doing something like this?"

"Not too many people. At least nobody whose name I know." Surprisingly, he was beginning to smile.

"What does that look mean?"

"You've taught me well, Shar." He reached into a zippered jacket pocket and drew out a small tape cassette.

"What's that?"

"A recording of a phone conversation. I went to my father's house the day before yesterday—presumably to see my mother, who's been sick. My father hasn't wanted me there, but he couldn't very well refuse Mom's request. Nor could he refuse it at lunchtime today, when she asked for me again. The bug that I planted on my father's phone in his den picked up his calls nicely—as did this tape."

I was stunned. Stunned and thrilled at what an exceptional operative Derek had turned into.

He added, "The voice on the tape has an accent I can't place. Maybe Hy should listen to it; he's good with languages." My husband spoke seven languages with some degree of fluency and had dabbled in several more.

I buzzed Hy's office and asked for him to join us.

7:27 p.m.

The voice on the tape was male, high pitched, and slightly accented. Its owner didn't identify himself to Martin Frye. "I assume everything with your son is under control," it said.

"…He'll do as I say."

The listener must have detected Frye's slight hesitation. "Are you certain of that?"

"The boy does as I say."

"He's hardly a boy. But I do suppose seventy-nine million, ten thousand two hundred forty-five dollars and some change is a strong incentive."

"You've been keeping close tabs on my accounts."

"And your son's."

"What's his is mine."

"I think not, Mr. Frye. As you've frequently complained, Derek is headstrong."

"He'll do as I say!"

"No need to get excited. When can we expect him to comply with our demands?"

"...I'm still negotiating that."

"In other words, he hasn't agreed."

Silence.

"And he may not agree to them at all."

"I said, I'm negotiating—"

"You have twenty-four hours, Martin. And then..."

"That's not enough time!"

"Twenty-three hours and fifty-nine minutes, Martin. Get to work."

The tape ended there.

Derek leaned back in his chair, letting his breath out explosively.

I looked at Hy. "That accent...?"

"Primarily Asian. Neither Chinese nor Japanese. One of the southeastern countries? No, I'd have picked up on that quickly. Filipino? Maybe. Play that tape again, please."

Derek played it. Hy shook his head, went to stare out

through the windows at the city lights. Then he snapped his fingers. "I've got it. The accent is a regional dialect of Pilipino. Speaker's probably from Batangas or Quezon Province."

"You can tell all that from what little he said on the tape?" Derek asked.

"I spent some time in the area back in my young and wild days." Hy winked at me. Only I and a few other people—most of whom were now dead—knew just how wild those days had been. "You're certain it was your father he was speaking to?"

Derek nodded, as if he'd taken a heavy weight onto his shoulders.

"Then you know what you need to do."

"Yeah."

We were silent for a while, the three of us looking out at the city lights, now winking through a swath of rain.

I said, "Would it help if we made it an official interview?"

"You mean, if you or Hy went along?"

"Yes."

"It might." Once again he was silent, considering.

"That way you might get better results by taking the personal aspect out of it," Hy said. "You know—'My colleague and I are here as part of a semiofficial inquiry. As a courtesy to you, we're asking our questions before officials enter the case and things get uncomfortable. Maybe we can find a way of keeping this from going public.'"

"God. I never thought I'd have the nerve to stand up to the old man that way, but I think with the help of one of you, I can."

"Which one?"

His eyes moved from Hy's to mine. "Shar would be best. My father is put off balance by assertive women. If I came in there with the two of you, it would be overkill." He smiled wryly. "An odd term for having a frank conversation with my own dad."

I looked at my watch. "Is it too late to talk with him tonight?"

"Nope. He's a night owl and proud of it."

"Then give the old owl a call."

8:01 p.m.

The Frye home was in Atherton, down the Peninsula, one of the most expensive suburbs in the Bay Area as well as the entire state. Winding hilltop lanes, expansive wooded acres, imposing homes with lights shielded behind high walls and ornate gates. I'd known Derek had been born into wealth and created more himself; he certainly lived well and denied himself few pleasures. But this display of opulence startled me. As Derek swung his Corvette up to a box and keyed in a code to make the gates open, I saw an interesting side of him.

The gates swung open and he steered the 'Vette along a driveway that curved through a thick stand of pines. Two other cars were parked in front of a floodlit white house: a Mercedes sedan and a heavy-duty SUV. Derek groaned.

"Shit," he said. "Dad's called in the reinforcements—his primary lawyer and the head of his company's security detail."

"Oh my, are we really that scary?"

He grinned at me. "He's gonna like you, McCone. He won't want to, but he will."

We were met at the door by a uniformed maid. Was she also one of the "reinforcements"? Apparently not a hostile one, considering the hug she gave Derek. He introduced her as Mrs. Dana, me as his boss. She took our coats and said to me, "It's nice to meet somebody who can boss him around."

Turning to Derek, she added, "Now, *he*"—jerking her head toward closed double doors to our left—"could take some of that bossing, if you know what I mean."

"Loaded for bear, is he?" Derek said.

"Yeah. And he's got *his* bears to back him up."

Derek sighed. "Into the fray," he said, steering me toward the doors.

Inside was a library—at least that was what it was meant to be, although the floor-to-ceiling shelves held few books. Instead they were full of relics from various travels to faraway lands: China, Indonesia, India. Three men sat in red leather chairs before an unlit fireplace. One was easily recognizable as Derek's father: handsome, with silver-gray hair and keen blue eyes; the lawyer I picked out because of his platinum-framed glasses and crisp blue suit; the third man was bald, thin lipped, and red nosed, dressed in expensive casual wear. I recognized him as Winslow Lambert. Introductions were made—the lawyer's name was Alfred Bastian—and Derek and I sat on a matching leather sofa.

I regarded Winslow Lambert. I hadn't seen him in some time, but he'd changed very little. His mannerisms were skittish, as if he were perpetually afraid of being attacked. His hands played restlessly with the cuffs of his jacket. His pale gaze jumped from place to place, never resting long on any one object. I wondered how much of his surroundings he was actually seeing.

Martin Frye took the lead, saying to his son, "I hope you'll be stopping upstairs to speak with your mother once we get this business out of the way."

"I'd planned on that. Once we're through."

"Well, now, what is it?"

"Ms. McCone will explain—"

"You set up this ill-timed meeting. You explain."

Frye hadn't looked at me since the introductions. I said, "I have a more comprehensive view of the case. It's best if I begin our conversation, sir."

The "sir" was something I'd learned way back in my career. It seemed to calm testy males.

Frye slowly nodded.

I said, "The case centers around real estate investment trusts. One in particular—WHS, upon whose board you're a director."

At the mention of WHS, Winslow Lambert's head jerked, and then, with an effort, he held it still, as if he were trying very hard to listen.

Frye said, "Information about that particular trust is closely held—"

"It might have remained closely held until someone on the board brought down a woman from the Pacific Northwest to manage it—Theresa Segretti, who resides on Rowan Court in Presidio Heights. I haven't been able to ascertain what Ms. Segretti's duties are; in fact, another board member whom I've spoken with, Glenn Solomon, was not aware of her existence."

At my mention of Glenn's name, Martin Frye's facial muscles tensed, and he glanced quickly at his attorney.

Alfred Bastian said, "Mr. Solomon is only nominally a board member. He very seldom attends meetings and isn't qualified to speak of WHS's other members or policies."

Martin Frye looked increasingly uncomfortable at Bastian's pronouncement. I went on swiftly to take advantage of it.

"From what I know of Ms. Segretti, she has no qualifi-cations for handling what's obviously a complicated land trust. Her background is primarily in running wilderness tours in partnership with a man named Gilbert Jacoby. She broke from Jacoby when she moved down here, but he followed her. Both, I believe, are users of hard drugs."

The attorney, Alfred Bastian, said, "Upon what do you base that allegation?"

"Their behavior, and Ms. Segretti's connection to a man who until last week ran a meth lab in the city."

Bastian and Frye exchanged glances. Lambert said, "The explosion on Russian Hill?"

"Right."

"Didn't someone die in that?"

"No. The perpetrator fled the city and…died elsewhere."

"In a drug burn?"

"The authorities haven't determined the cause yet."

"And this Ms. Segretti? What does she say?"

"Unfortunately, we haven't been able to locate her in the past twenty-four hours."

Martin Frye said impatiently, "What does all this have to do with me?"

"Glenn Solomon has named you as one of the principal shareholders in WHS. I'm planning to speak with all of them, but we won't know of their involvement in the illicit activities of the trust until I've completed that." I turned to Derek. "You may as well tell them what you discovered."

He produced his mini recorder from his pocket and played the tape. His father's face grew mottled with rage as he heard himself speaking to the unidentified caller about his son. "You placed a listening device in my own home!" he exclaimed. "Is this what that woman"—motioning to me—"and her agency have taught you?"

"She and the agency haven't taught me anything that I didn't already know—respect for the truth. Something that's sorely missing in this household."

Frye and his two associates sat silent.

To avoid a useless contretemps, I said, "We'll do what we can to prevent this situation from going public. But to accomplish that, I need a name."

"A name? What the hell do you mean?"

"The name of the man you were speaking with on that tape."

"The hell you'll get it!"

"We already know quite a bit. He's Filipino and his accent is regional. He's most likely a native of Batangas or Quezon Province."

Now Frye's face whitened, and he clutched the arms of his chair with rigid fingers. "Alfred?" he said to his attorney.

The man shook his head. "We can put off telling her, but that would be a delaying tactic at best."

"If the information gets out, it'll ruin me in the city."

"I'll try to cut you the best deal I can, Martin, but my guess is that you're already ruined in the city. And certainly with your son."

"I need to think! I need time!"

Derek said, "Thirty minutes, max. I'm going upstairs to see Mom. Come with, Shar?"

Gratefully, I nodded.

8:41 p.m.

Nara Frye was a petite woman wrapped in a pink silk robe, her gray-black hair secured in a bun on the top of her head.

A protracted illness—Derek had never been specific about its nature—had taken a toll on her fine features, but I could see that she'd once been a beauty. In contrast to her recent years as a wealthy Atherton matron, her early life had not been easy.

She'd been born in Tule Lake Relocation Camp, where many of California's Japanese—whether citizens or not—had been interned during World War II. She'd weathered the effects of what many of us considered our state's greatest shame and, orphaned and released into the city at sixteen, had gone to work in the garment industry sweatshops at night while pursuing a business degree by day at SF State. There she'd met Martin Frye, a former marine studying on the GI Bill, and she had aided him over the years in establishing his wholesale grocery business. Having now met Martin Frye, I assumed none of those years had been easy.

Nara reached up from the recliner where she sat before a glowing fireplace to embrace her son, then took both my hands warmly.

"Your business with your father is finished?" she asked Derek.

"Nearly."

"He didn't take it well?"

"No."

She sighed. "It's been a long time coming."

I glanced at Derek in surprise. He said, "She's always known about what we used to call Dad's business tricks. Neither of us suspected until recently how much damage to his associates and others those tricks have done."

"There will be no more." She shook her head firmly.

Derek balanced on the arm of her chair, his hand on her cheek. "What will you do, Mom?"

"What I've always done—go on. I learned long ago not to fight him. Maybe now that you're doing that job for me, there will be some peace in this house."

"You could always come to me—"

She pushed his hand away playfully. "Oh, sure—have Mama-san living in your bachelor's roost, or whatever people call them nowadays, spoiling all your fun. No, I'll take my chances with the old rooster."

I faded away toward the door to give them privacy. Maybe sometimes things did work out.

8:57 p.m.

We sped back toward the city on Highway 280, the eight-lane expanse lightly traveled, headlights and taillights trailing streamers through the mist. Derek steered the 'Vette steadily; his face, which had been agonized only hours before, was now curiously at peace. He'd suspected the truth, and acceptance had already set in.

We now had a full explanation of the private-streets scheme. Martin Frye, Winslow Lambert, and Benjamin Aspirillo—who had been the man speaking with Martin Frye on Derek's tape—had conspired with Theresa Segretti to have several small streets vandalized in order to drive down their value and buy them up at fire-sale prices. They would then enter into an agreement with foreign developers, the new mayor-elect, and corrupt members of the city planning commission to develop them as luxury residences that would sell for many millions. The revelation of their scheme would rattle cages all over the city and shake the local power structure to its foundations.

I began making calls, gathering the team to the agency. None were surprised at the lateness of the hour or the suddenness of the summons. None objected at being yanked from their evening pursuits. Over the years I'd assembled a good group of people around me; the moments when a difficult case came together were what we lived for.

The agency was abuzz when our elevator arrived at the top floor.

Courtesy of Mick, pots of coffee and tea brewed on a cart outside the conference room. From outside, the room looked like a sleek executive gathering place: wide interior and exterior windows, miniblinds, plush carpeting, comfy leather chairs. But in its center sat the agency's most treasured relic: the battered oak round table that had once graced (or should I say disgraced?) the area before the kitchen windows at All Souls. We're a sentimental bunch, those of us who thrashed out the details of many a case over this table, and we've passed the sentiment along to those who joined in after us.

Around the table I saw that many people were already seated: Patrick Neilan; Hank, whom I'd asked, as our lawyer, to be here; Julia Rafael, back from her long leave of absence; Zoe Anderson; Natalie Su; Hy; and a couple of operatives from his side. I was surprised not to see Ted, who relished these impromptu conferences, but Mick had told me he'd called in sick.

I took a mug of coffee (mine says "Boss Woman") and went to my place at the table, where someone had once scratched "McCone Rules" (next to which someone had more recently scratched "Ripinsky"). There were other inscriptions, some now fading, others freshly incised into the wood. They expressed the participants' opinions on global concerns

("No Nukes"), politics ("Trump Sucks"), the environment ("Save the Whales"), and race ("Black Lives Matter"), as well as the strictly personal (initials in hearts, some crossed out).

When everybody had settled down, I said, "We have two principal motivators behind the vandalisms, plus a rationale for them. It's up to us to figure out the best way to proceed."

Hy looked up from the scratch pad in front of him. He'd been doodling on it when I came in, but now his eyes met mine keenly.

I went on, "The first motivator is Winslow Lambert. You may remember him as the activist who founded People for Equitable Housing." Rae, drawing on her store of housing problems in the city, had refreshed my memory about Lambert's activities when I called her during our drive up from Atherton. The organization had been highly touted by our former mayor as a solution to the difficulties of housing for the working poor, but it had then been dissolved as costly and unnecessary by the present mayor. Lambert, known as a rabble-rouser, had railed at the decision and threatened radical reprisals but ultimately faded from the city scene. Now he was back, but in a less official role.

The group around the table nodded and scratched notes.

I went on, "Lambert isn't admitting it, but it's likely he's been working behind the scenes, promoting the vandalisms with Theo Segretti and another cohort, Benjamin Aspirillo. Aspirillo is a Filipino entrepreneur who is working sub rosa to buy up prime city real estate at rock-bottom prices to develop as luxury accommodations. He has at least two silent partners here in the Bay Area: Martin Frye, Derek's father, and our mayor-elect."

Murmurs, then silence.

"We have signed statements from Martin Frye and his attorney. Aspirillo has denied everything through his lawyer. Segretti and Gilbert Jacoby have disappeared but should be located momentarily. What we need to do is decide how to release our information."

More murmurs: "To the press, as soon as possible." "Crucify the mayor-elect and the garbage that supported him." "Sorry, Derek, but your father's real bad news."

Derek stared steadily at the speaker.

I held up my hand. "This is not about Martin Frye and his associates. Or even Jacoby and his vandalisms. The question is: Can we influence how this story will affect the good of the city?"

"But the people's right to *know*!" Patrick's tone was sarcastic. He was not a fan of the fourth estate.

"They'll know, soon enough." I looked at Hank. "You're in tight with the mayor. Will you inform her of our ongoing progress and seek assistance?"

"Of course."

"The SFPD?" Patrick asked.

"They haven't been notified yet and won't be until we have more information on Aspirillo and WHS's activities. I'll leave it to the rest of you to divide them up and proceed. Glenn Solomon has indicated he'll be willing to assist."

Willing? He'd wanted to jump in running.

"What about you?" Patrick asked. "What'll you be doing?"

"Coordinating with everyone. Rae will assist, and Julia has agreed to help."

"Hy, are you in on this?" Patrick asked.

"Yes, as long as I'm not called out on another case."

"You'll both be here in the offices?"

"Or easily reachable."

9:38 p.m.

When we left the conference room, I noticed someone being held under guard by two operatives in a smaller interview room: Gilbert Jacoby. He looked even worse than the last time I'd seen him: hair snarled, cheeks stubbled, wearing clothing that was close to rags. I went up to the ops—Bill Allen and Tony Cruz—and asked what he was doing here.

Tony said, "He showed up at Rowan Court about an hour ago. Gave us a hell of a fight—high and belligerent, yelling for Segretti. We had to subdue him. Then we offered him the opportunity to be escorted here or to the SFPD. After that he didn't put up much of a protest."

"I'll talk to him shortly. Anything on Segretti?"

Bill replied, "I think you may have already read my report, but to recap, she appeared at the house about an hour before Jacoby did. Went out to where she garages her car on Van Ness. I was assigned to tail her, so I followed her across town to the Bay Bridge but lost her in a traffic jam caused by a multicar pileup."

Wonderful San Francisco traffic. "I'll talk with Jacoby now."

He gave me a feeble glance when I entered the room, then looked away. "So you've decided to cooperate," I said.

Shrug.

"Why'd you go to Rowan Court? To reconcile with Segretti?"

"Thought she'd give me some of her money."

"Why would she do that? She doesn't strike me as generous, and the two of you are through anyway."

"We're not through if I say we're not. Anyway, she's always got money. It's the reason she came down here to work with that WHS outfit—to steal from them."

"How do you know that?"

"That's what she does—steals."

"How much money did she take from WHS?"

"I don't know. A lot."

As if the information gods were smiling on me, Mick stepped through the door and handed me a slip of paper. It said, "$847,219.17. Cash."

Glenn had promised to go over the WHS accounts and had apparently gotten right on it.

I said to Mick, "A significant amount like that, she must have been skimming it over quite some time."

"Glenn's sending an email with the dates of the withdrawals. It's been going on close to two months."

"Too bad neither he nor anybody else on that board bothered to monitor the accounts. Withdrawals like that, even over a long period of time, would have tipped them to what was going on."

"Benign neglect."

"No, stupidity." I turned to Gil Jacoby. "Is there anything else you can tell us about Theresa Segretti?"

"Yeah—she's a bitch. When we were partners in the wilderness tour business, I thought she was a pretty cool person. But it turned out she was sucking up to our rich clients for money. That was when she connected with this WHS guy—Aspirillo, I think his name is. Said he needed someone to orchestrate things, act as a buffer with the coalition or whatever. Don't know what he offered her to come down here, but it had to be a lot. That's what Theo's all about—the big bucks."

"You searched the house on Rowan Court thoroughly for money?"

"Not as thoroughly as I wanted to. Your goons busted in there and roughed me up. I oughta sue. I'm thinking about it."

Everybody wants to sue—for everything.

I said, "Mr. Jacoby, I'd like to offer you a stay in one of our hospitality suites." We maintained two in the building, originally for clients who had reason to fear for their safety, but more and more lately for witnesses we didn't want walking around on their own.

"You arresting me?"

"If I wanted you held officially, I'd be calling the cops. I'm offering to put you up so you'll be available for further questioning. As far as I can tell, you haven't done anything actionable."

He looked puzzled; he probably didn't know what "actionable" meant.

"This suite," he asked, "what's it like?"

I suppressed a sigh. "Comfortable."

"Minibar?"

"Yes."

"Room service?"

"You can order up from the deli downstairs."

"It's a deal."

I didn't mention the guard who would be posted on the door in case he decided to sneak out.

10:12 p.m.

"Over three-quarters of a million dollars," Hy said. We were sitting in the empty conference room, drinking the dregs of the coffee. "According to the schedule of withdrawals that Glenn just sent over, the last occurred on Wednesday. Why didn't Segretti take off with it then?"

"Maybe she had preparations to make. She might have been redepositing it into other accounts."

"Where, though?"

"Good question. I guess it depends on where she planned to go."

"She'd have been well advised to get far away from here."

"Maybe. Or maybe…"

"What?"

"Let me think on it a moment."

He waited. I turned to look out the window.

"Maybe," I said again, "Segretti didn't have the money. Maybe someone else took it away from her."

"Who could've done that?"

"The same person who took her diamond ring."

"Sam Sage."

"Yes. Sam had his eye on a lot of scams. Maybe he suspected that Davis Segretti didn't exist and was attempting to blackmail Theo by exposing her as a fraud and holding up her activities to police scrutiny."

"And what would she have done then?"

"What victims have been doing to blackmailers since time immemorial."

Hy thought on it, nodded. "We need more facts before we go off on this tangent."

"So let's collect them—"

There was a commotion in the reception room. A male voice yelling. We went out there.

Winslow Lambert was prancing around. His eyes were wide and snapping, his fists balled, and the redness of his nose had bled out to suffuse most of his face. I could make out only parts of what he was shouting: "...ruining my life...busybody broad...I wanna kill her..."

I stepped forward, said, "Mr. Lambert, what *is* the problem?"

He whirled, one balled fist nearly connecting with my shoulder. I turned to Hy and said, "Can you put him in the conference room?"

But Lambert seemed determined to continue creating a scene. His feet churned, then gained purchase on the carpet, and he was off and running—quite inexplicably, down the hall toward my office. Two of the operatives who had been watching his performance went after him.

I said, "I don't need this. I *so* don't need this."

There was a thump at the end of the hall and then quiet.

I glanced anxiously at Hy. "Those guys wouldn't really have hurt him, would they?"

"Don't know. *I* would've."

"Me too."

Tony Cruz, the first op, returned and said, "He tripped and connected with a doorjamb. Isn't badly hurt, but seems worn out. We have him on the couch in your office, Ms. McCone."

"Good. Keep him there till I can decide what to do with him."

Hy said, "He probably needs medical attention. I'll call Doc Robinson."

Since the old days with RKI, he'd availed himself of the services of a doctor who made house calls in irregular circumstances.

11:01 p.m.

I went back into the conference room. My eyes felt gritty, as if they'd been sandpapered. My temples pounded. I took three aspirins from my bag and washed them down with warm water from a carafe on the table, which was littered with reports, printouts of emails, and crumpled papers.

Hy came in and said, "Doc'll be here shortly."

"Good." I sat down, looked at a tablet where I'd scribbled some notes. "Suppose Theo converted the money into cash and was ready to leave town, but had an altercation with Sam, and he took off with it. Segretti could've conducted the same kind of property search Derek did, found out about the place near Red Bluff, and gone there hoping to recoup her losses."

"And then she killed him. The background checks on her show she owns a Beretta. One flaw, though: Wouldn't she have grabbed the money and disappeared then, rather than come back to the city?"

I frowned. "She might have—unless she didn't get hold of it. Maybe Sam had it hidden someplace where she couldn't find it. But why would she shoot him before he gave it up?"

"Maybe he refused; he was a pretty determined son of a bitch. He could have tried to take the gun away from her and it went off. Or she could have shot him in a rage when he wouldn't tell her where the money was. Drug addicts are unstable."

"But she had all the time in the world to search for it after she drove his body down to that stream in his truck."

Then I thought back to a time years ago—the first time I'd ever shot someone. It had been justified—I'd fired to save a friend's life—but in the split second after I'd seen my victim's body crumple, I'd wanted to run as fast as I could from the scene and the fact that I'd killed another human being. Segretti could have felt the same way.

I said, "She might have gone into shock and decided to get away from there before somebody came and found her."

"And intended to come back and hunt for the money later."

"Right. But then I found Sam's body and, with the police presence, she couldn't return right away. But by now enough time has passed so she'd feel safe enough to go back to Gray's Landing. That would explain where she was headed when she drove across the Bay Bridge yesterday."

"She won't still be there if she found the money."

"But she will be if she's still searching."

Hy said, "You sure there's no way you can check to see if she's on the property?"

"There's no phone, no near neighbors. No reason to call on the sheriff's department with a bunch of suppositions; they couldn't legally act on what we told them. Probably wouldn't believe us if we did. I know the Realtor who's handling the listing for the property, but I'm not going to involve her in a potentially dangerous situation."

"So it's up to us."

"You and me."

"We can fly up there..."

"And I can get the woman from Econocar to bring a

rental to the airport. We'll drive out, check the place, see if Segretti's there."

"She'll be armed."

"So will we."

There was a tap on the window. Doc Robinson's wrinkled face peered in at us. Hy went to speak with him, then came back. "He'll take care of Lambert," he told me.

"Think we should fly up to Red Bluff right away?" I asked.

"Why not? We can check out the farm in the dark. If Segretti's there, we'll tackle her at first light."

"Okay." I took out my phone, called the number for Econocar. I expected to reach a machine, but Emmy answered.

"Sure, I can have a Jeep ready for you. Just call me from the airfield."

"It'll be the middle of the night."

"In my spare time I'm a college student," she said. "I don't sleep all that much anyway."

Doc Robinson appeared again. Hy conferred with him, came back. "Lambert's in bad shape. Doc's going to have him admitted to SF General. An ambulance is on the way."

"Good. Let's get out of here in case Lambert goes on another rampage when he sees the EMTs."

WEDNESDAY, NOVEMBER 9

12:39 a.m.

We preflighted the plane in record time and took off into the dark when the Oakland ATC gave us clearance. Small beacons and traffic signals were winking along the Peninsula and across the East Bay, but most residences and businesses remained dark.

After a while, a light rain began, drops streaking across the contours of the plane's windscreen. The air in the cabin felt stuffy and clammy. I drank from the go-cup of coffee that I'd gotten from a machine in the pilots' lounge and passed it on to Hy, then undid the clasps on my flight jacket and wriggled around in the seat, trying to get comfortable.

Emmy from the rental car company was waiting when we landed at the airport, looking cheerful despite the hour.

"More trouble out there?" she asked.

"Just checking on a few things," I said, and introduced her to Hy.

"You want the sheriff?"

"No." Not yet, anyway.

"Well, you know where to reach me if you need anything."

The rain had let up but began again as we drove through

Gray's Landing and then along the rutted road through the orchards. A quarter mile along the drive to the farmhouse, where it curved and a grove of pine trees blocked a view of the old house, I brought the Jeep to a stop. We got out and made our way to where we could view the dooryard without being seen by anyone in or near the house. Our flashlights showed deep tire tracks in the muddy ground from the vehicles that had come after I'd found Sam Sage's body. There was no sign of a pale-green Volvo or any other car, but Hy's sharp eye picked out what appeared to be fresh tracks.

"A car drove in here within the last twenty-four hours," he said. "Doesn't look as if it's come back out."

"Then where is it?"

"In the barn, judging by the direction of the tracks."

"Nobody's outside anywhere, and there're no visible lights in the house, but if Segretti's still here, she must be inside."

"Or in the barn with the car."

We detoured through the pines until the barn was between us and the house. Still nothing was moving anywhere as we crossed to the near side of the barn, where a broken window afforded a look inside. I boosted myself up and craned my neck. The pale-green, late-model Volvo was there, but Segretti wasn't. I gave Hy a thumbs-up sign and slipped down.

"She has to be in the house," I said.

"Sleeping or still searching for the money, probably. She wouldn't just be sitting around doing nothing."

"Unless she's high."

"Which would make her even more dangerous if she's

armed, and she's bound to be. We can't take a chance going to the house directly or around to the rear. Too much open ground; she might see us if she's near a window or hear us before we can get inside. Best option is to draw her out into the open."

I agreed. "What we need is a diversion. How about something that would threaten her car—her only means of escape."

"Good. A fire, nothing dangerous, just a small smoky one. That ought to be enough to bring her outside."

"There must be something in the barn we can use to start one."

Hy boosted me through the window this time, swung himself in behind me, and switched on his flashlight. There was a workbench, a few rusted tools scattered on its dusty surface; a pegboard, a few more tools hanging on hooks; a jumble of rakes, shovels, and hoes. An old broken-down tractor that looked as if it hadn't been run in decades. Bales and loose piles of rotting hay filled one corner next to a big carton of fossilized insecticide.

Hy said, "If some of that hay is dry enough, we can use it and the insecticide to start the kind of fire we need. Set it where we can put it out quickly if we have to."

"What'll we light it with? Neither of us carries matches."

"There's a lantern hooked on that beam near the doors. Might be matches there."

There weren't, but luckily we found a small box of wooden matches in a drawer in the workbench.

Most of the loose hay was damp and moldy, but we uncovered a few armloads that would be dry enough to burn. We carried them to the closed barn doors. The doors weren't locked; we opened one of them a few inches and I peered out at the house. Still no sign of Segretti.

We stacked the hay in front of the opening. When we had enough, Hy dumped some of the insecticide on top. I said, "Where'll we go to watch for her? Back into the trees?"

"Yes, but only far enough for a view of the house and yard. There's brush at the edge of the grove where we can hunker down, if you don't mind a few brambles."

"That's the last thing I'd mind right now."

We went through the grove to find a vantage point, then sat down with our arms around one another and huddled in our flight jackets to wait for first light. I must have dozed because I was startled by the caw of a crow and opened my eyes to gray morning.

"What time is it?" I asked.

"Nearly seven. Let me check on the house."

Hy slipped away through the brush. I stood, trying to work the stiffness out of my back and shoulders.

In a moment Hy returned. "Segretti's awake. There's a light on in one of the side windows. Let's go."

We went back inside the barn. Hy struck a match and tossed it into the hay. When the stuff started to smoke, we hurried across to the window, climbed out, and ran through the pines and into our place in the brush. Hy took his .45 from his shoulder holster, checked its load. I took out my .38 and did the same.

Acrid gray smoke had begun to puff out through the partially open barn door. In the stillness I could hear the faint crackling of the fire inside. In three or four minutes the smell of the smoke grew thick. Then the door to the house flew open and Segretti came charging out.

She darted toward the barn, her attention focused there and her right arm hanging down against her hip. I should have known she was armed, but with the smoke roiling around her as she neared the barn doors, I didn't see the small-caliber handgun clutched in her hand until Hy and I stepped out of the brush with our weapons extended.

The distance between her and us was no more than twenty yards when I shouted, "Stop right there, Segretti! Drop the gun!"

She staggered at the sound of my voice, her head swiveling toward us, squinting through the smoke. But she didn't obey the command. Instead she twisted around in our direction, lifted her arm, and squeezed off two rapid shots. The first one was wild, but the second wasn't, dammit— I heard Hy grunt and go down. But he wasn't badly hurt; he rolled over, grimacing, hunching his left shoulder and struggling to bring up his .45.

I saw that at a quick glance, my attention mostly focused on Segretti. "Drop it, damn you!" I yelled at her. "Drop it!"

She didn't obey that command either. Crouching, she fired a third shot, that one closer than the first.

I didn't hesitate. I shot her in the forehead, just where she'd shot Sam Sage.

THURSDAY, NOVEMBER 10

We were airborne in Two-Seven-Tango heading south for Oakland. I piloted. Hy lounged in the passenger seat, his left arm in a sling. He'd been given a prescription for Percodan and was half-asleep.

His shoulder wound wasn't serious. He'd said as much, to my relief, when I ran to him after the shooting. I'd immediately called the sheriff's department, reported what had happened, and requested an EMT unit. Hy had been standing, more or less steady on his feet, when I finished the call. He refused my offer to help him across the yard to the house, saying, "I can make it on my own. You check on Segretti and do something about that fire before the whole damn barn goes up."

A quick look at the bloody bullet hole in Segretti's forehead had confirmed that she was dead. Unlike the first time I'd killed someone, I hadn't felt the urge to run away, and I'd felt no remorse at having had to kill Segretti, just a flat, dull heaviness. I'd experience more repercussions later; violence, no matter how necessary, always leaves a grim residue.

Smoke had still been billowing out through the barn door, but not as thickly, and there were no visible flames. I dragged one door all the way open, then did the same with the other. The fire, smoldering by then, had done no more than scorch the inside of the doors, and the damp, moldy hay had kept it from flaring and spreading. I kicked the burning straw out into the yard, stomped on it until all the fire was out.

Hy had made it across the yard and was sitting on the porch steps. I joined him, and we sat there waiting for the sheriff and his deputies and the EMT unit.

It had been only a few minutes before they arrived. After answering the sheriff's questions, and while the EMTs were dressing Hy's wound, I'd gone to fetch the Jeep. We'd driven into town to the sheriff's department, where further explanations of the chaotic scene at the farm went on for hours. Exhausted and on edge as we were, we'd decided to stay the night at the Golden Hills Motel.

After we'd checked in, I called the agency. Mick told me that Hank had met with the current mayor and that the mayor-elect was being questioned as to his part in the private-streets scheme. Martin Frye and Benjamin Aspirillo had surrounded themselves with legal teams, and Winslow Lambert was resting quietly at SF General. Gilbert Jacoby was now in police custody and talking freely to SFPD and SFFD inspectors. The PD would coordinate its efforts with those of Red Bluff authorities. A press conference had been called at city hall; did I wish to join in? I respectfully declined.

This morning I'd checked in with the county authorities, and Sheriff's Deputy Bud Wentz had informed me that the handgun Segretti had fired at us was the same type of .32 Beretta that had been used to kill Sam Sage; ballistics reports were pending, not that the obvious results were needed. As for the missing money, apparently Segretti hadn't found it, and so far neither had the sheriff's men who were combing the farm property. Sam Sage had hidden it well, maybe too well. It might never be found.

The Percodan Hy had taken was starting to wear off. He stirred in his seat and said, "Well, McCone, this sure has been one of our more stressful experiences."

"I'm glad it's over. I hope to God I never have another like it."

"Vacation."

"What?"

"We need a vacation."

"That we do," I agreed.

As if in response to his suggestion, my cell vibrated. I removed my headset and put the phone on speaker. Hy leaned over to listen.

"Shar?" Ted's voice, slightly distorted. "Where are you guys?"

"Flying home from an outing." I wasn't about to explain now all that had happened over the past few days.

"Glad I caught you. Feel like another?"

"To where?"

"Where I'm calling from. Hawaii—the Big Island."

"What're you doing there?"

"Planning a wedding. I took your advice and flew over to Tokyo. Found Neal and dragged him to a friend's vacation house here. We hashed out our problems—some I didn't even know we had—and decided to take the big step."

"Great!" I exclaimed.

"Congratulations," Hy said.

"How soon can you get here?"

"As soon as we can get home, book a commercial flight, and pick up a change of clothes."

"Wedding's super casual. Lots of friends are coming. They all say—"

Hy and I smiled at each other.

"They all say they need a vacation," we finished for him.

Afterword

Ted Smalley and Neal Osborn were married in Puako on Hawaii's Big Island. Sharon, Hy, and many of M&R's staff attended, enjoying much-needed vacations.

Rae Kelleher and Ricky Savage's Go Home Foundation has so far provided 1,473 residences for the homeless and working poor in San Francisco.

Hank Zahn and his daughter, Habiba Hamid, continue to spar over living arrangements in their Noe Valley home.

Derek Frye successfully sued for control of his multimillion-dollar trust fund and is setting up a program to train underprivileged students in technological skills.

Julia Rafael has returned to M&R after a yearlong hiatus to aid Patrick Neilan in scheduling operatives' assignments. A romance is brewing between the two.

Mick Savage fell in love with a winemaker whom he met on an excursion to the Sonoma Valley. A spring wedding is planned.

Sharon and Hy continue to investigate, live, and love in San Francisco.

About the Author

Marcia Muller has written many novels and short stories. She has won six Anthony Awards and a Shamus Award and is also the recipient of the Private Eye Writers of America's Lifetime Achievement Award as well as the Mystery Writers of America Grand Master Award (their highest accolade). She lives in northern California with her husband, mystery writer Bill Pronzini.

LOOKING FOR MORE SHARON McCONE?

TURN THE PAGE FOR A PREVIEW OF
MARCIA MULLER'S *ICE AND STONE*.

NEW YORK TIMES BESTSELLING AUTHOR

Marcia
Muller

ICE AND
STONE

A SHARON McCONE MYSTERY

AVAILABLE NOW

SATURDAY, JANUARY 5

4:13 p.m.

From its rim at the side of Fisher's Mill Road, the deadfall looked treacherous: sand-colored boulders, felled trees, tangled dead branches, moraines of rock and sediment spilling down to the river below. I hefted my cumbersome backpack, looked dubiously at the walking stick that my guide, Allie Foxx, had provided to help me keep my balance.

Yeah, sure—I'll probably still end up on my ass.

Allie was already halfway down the slope. She made a hurry-up sign to me. I closed my eyes and started off.

Closing my eyes was not the smartest thing I'd ever done: my work boots skittered over a patch of stones, a branch whopped me on the forehead, and I came to rest leaning against a birdlimed outcropping.

When I looked down the slope, I saw Allie had turned her back. She was probably hiding laughter. Her tribe, the Meruk, I'd read, did not believe in ridiculing others.

Well, I had to admit I must look ridiculous: clumsy in my overstuffed cold-weather clothing, red faced and sweating in spite of the icy wind. But dedicated— oh yes.

I'd been hired the previous week by the Eureka-based Crimes against Indigenous Sisters organization to investigate why two Native women had been murdered in Meruk County over the past three months as well as look into many prior disappearances. The cases were not localized: Indigenous women have long been victims of mysterious crimes in areas from Arizona to the far reaches of Canada, from the Sierra Nevada to the Pacific. But Meruk and its surrounding counties—Del Norte, Tehama, Siskiyou, and Modoc—had experienced an ominous uptick in such crimes, and CAIS wanted to know why. So did I.

I straightened, set my backpack more firmly on my shoulders, and started off again. This time the going was easier and, except for a couple of near falls, I made it upright to where Allie was now waiting on the bank of the Little White River. To her left the water flowed free from under an ancient arched stone bridge, but to her right the river became choked by more downed trees, dead grasses, and boulders. I slid toward her on a pebbled patch of ice.

She smiled, her white teeth a sharp contrast to her brown, weathered skin. "We'll make a cross-country tracker of you yet, Sharon."

"Cross-country catastrophe is more like it."

"Nah, you just need a little more practice." Her expression became serious. "This cell phone is for you. As I mentioned before, none work here except those signed up with the local provider, and, at that, the reception is spotty. You may have to go into the village to make any calls."

"Thanks. I take it Internet service is just as bad."

"Worse, I'm afraid. You won't have a vehicle for a couple

of days, but the village is walkable, and I've arranged with my brother who has a car dealership in the county seat to have a Jeep delivered to you. The shack is fully stocked, and anything you need, just give a call. You have your keys?"

"Yes. And my instructions and my lists."

"Sorry to sound like an overprotective mama, but I was one for a lot of years. Be careful on that ledge under the bridge, it's slippery. Once you're on the other side, you turn left—"

"Yes, Mom."

"And in an emergency, you'll—"

"I know."

"Okay. This is where I leave you. The killer, or killers, might recognize me, given the publicity the organization's been getting. I'll put as much distance between us as possible." She squeezed my arm, turned, and walked quickly uphill.

I was on my own.

The narrow ledge under the bridge *was* slippery, but I had the walking stick for balance. Even through my thick boots I could feel the iciness of the water, and sharp stones poked against their soles. The arching bridge wall felt clammy and smelled of mold. Rustling sounds accompanied my passage, and I thought of bats.

And then I was out on the far side. The light was fading, so I flicked on my small flash before proceeding. I scrambled left up the mud-slick slope, past a jumbled pile of rocks and there—

There it was.

The old abandoned shack belonging to the Sisters was

built of redwood that had weathered to a dull silver gray. Its windows were nailed shut with many sheets of plywood and crisscrossing timbers; tattered black shingles lay loose on its roof, some littering the ground. The single door was secured by a rusted chain and an odd-looking padlock. It seemed as if no one had entered it in decades.

But I knew better.

The padlock was difficult, even though Allie had given me a demonstration when she'd handed me the key. One prong of the key had to be inserted at an angle, another pushed up from below. When I pulled, nothing happened; I removed and reinserted the key, pressed harder, pulled again. There was a faint click, and the staple released. I removed the padlock and the chain, pulled the door open, and stepped inside.

Under other circumstances I would have expected dust, cobwebs, and stale odors, but instead a pleasant, flowery scent came to my nostrils. Air freshener. I shone my light around the single room. Two lanterns sat on the big braided rug. I fumbled in my pocket for matches, lit one.

The light from the lantern was dim; I was pleased with that, even though Allie had told me that every chink between the old boards had been caulked to prevent telltale leakage. I set my pack down and looked around.

The structure had been built in the mid-1980s by a man who had inherited the land and hoped to turn it into a retreat for recovering alcoholics, but the extremes of weather and difficulty of hauling in construction supplies had defeated him, and he'd died—sadly, an alcoholic himself—in the early 2000s, willing the property to the Sisters, who had befriended him and nursed him in his final illness. They'd maintained the cabin as well as they could, but they'd been working against great odds. And now it seemed they'd worked hard at reclaiming it for me.

To my right, under the windows, was a bunk topped with an air mattress, a sleeping bag, and a big, fluffy pillow; to the left a tiny bathroom with a chemical toilet and small sink had been partitioned off from the rest of the room. Two jugs of water, foodstuffs, and other supplies were stowed beneath a wide shelf.

I eyed the comfortable-looking bunk. I was exhausted. Early that morning I'd flown my Cessna 170B from its base at Oakland Airport's North Field to a tiny paved strip at Bluefork over in Modoc County. The strip belonged to Hal Bascomb, one of my husband Hy's flying buddies, who had been sworn to secrecy about my presence in the area and had provided the loan of one of his three dilapidated Quonset hut hangars to shelter the plane. After we stowed the plane, Hal gave me a hand up into his Jeep. He looked good: sun browned and golden haired in spite of the time of year. Long ago he and Hy had worked together on some dodgy jobs in Southeast Asia, and they had been friends ever since. Now Hal claimed he was taking it easy, that running the strip in Bluefork was his retirement. But I could see that same steely look in his eyes that I occasionally glimpsed in Hy's. People in certain pursuits never quite retire.

Allie had met us on the outskirts of the nearby village of Aspendale in her Land Rover, and after a short drive she and I had arrived in Saint Germaine. An unincorporated and fairly unpopulated area, named after a long-abandoned monastery on the far side of the river, Saint Germaine was where the fatal attacks on two Indigenous women had occurred over the last three months. I'd have to—

Table that until tomorrow, McCone. You're too tired to think clearly now. Put on your sweats, crawl into that bunk, and get some sleep.